Duval Porter

The Poems of Duvall Porter

Duval Porter

The Poems of Duvall Porter

ISBN/EAN: 9783337407469

Printed in Europe, USA, Canada, Australia, Japan

Cover: Foto ©Andreas Hilbeck / pixelio.de

More available books at **www.hansebooks.com**

THE

POEMS

OF

ᗪUVALL ᖴORTER.

TO THE MEMORY OF

MY MOTHER,

THIS BOOK IS DEDICATED.

INTRODUCTION.

In keeping with a time-honored custom, we will detain the reader a few moments with an explanation of the book he is about to peruse. As Patrick Henry said, "it is natural for man to indulge in the illusions of hope," and it is more natural still for a writer of books to indulge in the same pleasant recreation, for we opine but few men enter literary life, without having, as they suppose, some data at least upon which to base their calculation of success. Furthermore, it has been truly said that the child of the mind is dearer than the child of the body, and we are inclined to believe the assertion true. The author, then, ventures upon this work with the usual alternations of hope and fear ; and while he will be gratified beyond measure should he succeed, and disappointed if he fails, he is too well aware, that whatever the estimate the reading public may put upon his work, that it is in the main, too, correct, to dispute its conclusions. As to the contents, a few words. The reader will find a variety of subjects treated, but the author has adopted that mode of versification best adapted to express his thoughts and ideas, and in consequence, he will not find that diffuseness of style and method, which is a distinguishing feature in the works of Tennyson. Most of the poems were written under strong conviction, and should the energy of the language used at certain passages, encroach upon the limits of taste, it is hoped that the purity of the motive may condone the want of a true regard for that refined and delicate sense.

With this, we commend our undertaking to a generous public, ever willing to bestow praise when deserved, and brave enough to deny it when undeserved.

THE AUTHOR.

CONTENTS.

NARRATIVE POEMS.

CRITICAL POEMS.

MISCELLANEOUS POEMS.

ALPHONSO:

A ROMANCE IN FOUR CANTOS.

Not far from whence, a sweet, majestic stream
E'er rolls its way in ceaseless monotone
Thro' fertile fields, where smiling harvests teem,
Till broad Atlantic claims it as its own,
Was born and rear'd the hero of my story,
Obscure, unknown and on no page of glory.

But e'en in youth he felt the hidden fire
Of genius, kindling in his eager mind,
And liv'd in realms, great souls alone desire,
And beauties saw, where darker souls were blind,
Fields, fruits and flowers, nurs'd that peculiar flame,
Which men call genius,—a thing without a name.

In youth he was a strange, abstracted being,
Dwelling in ideals, beauties only known
To him, whom Heaven, imparts the longing, seeing
Of hidden worlds, whose light has never shone
For souls unworthy, worms may dwell in dust
But genius never, dwell in heavens it must.

Oft was he seen, when blazing lightnings played
In shapes grotesque upon the angry cloud,
Ascend some steep, or lofty palisade,
And watch the tempest, the giant oaks that bowed
Their lofty tops, as though the sight conveyed
The latent storm, which in his bosom preyed.

Oh genius!! akin to madness as thou art,
Who, without rapture, could'st know thine early dream;
What, if from madness, but a hair's breadth apart,
Who knoweth but madness may with beauty teem
The tallest towers are they that soonest fall
The brilliant mind,—a maniac's for all.

The lofty mountain and deep ocean nurse
The soul of genius in its childish years,
But woman, nay love, commands from it the verse
That makes it human, baptises it in tears,
Imbuing it with ecstacy and feeling
Which Nature has no power of revealing.

'Tis the sad misfortune of poetic minds
To seek that here, which only dwells above,
Whose own effulgence, but too often blinds,
And, part creates, the object of its love,
Till alas; too late, an aching heart must feel
Ideals unworthy of its baffled zeal.

Love makes the poet, he cannot exist
Devoid of all its ecstacy and pain;
Love is the food on which he must subsist,
'Tis love supplies his sweet inspiring strain.
Rob him of this and jar and discord swell;
His highest heaven becomes his lowest hell.

Alphonso in his early youth did love
A being cast, he deem'd in beauty's mould,
And what earth lack'd he borrow'd from above,
Till she became the thing his fancy told.
Poetic minds, despite the sense of sight
Can frame perfection; what is wrong make right.

Fair Nature now, at once he quite forsook,
And made a truce with flowers, fields and skies
Save when anon he wander'd by the brook,
In pensive mood, or such as love supplies.
All passion, phantasy and fondness hers,
With all pure thought that early love first stirs.

Oh, Spirit of Love! full adequate art thou
To stir to action powers of the soul,
To create thoughts, that hence, no more, nor now
Shall sleep, or brook right reason's stern control.
An Eden brighter can lovers' mind create
Than Adam knew ere he received his mate.

One master-passion of the human breast
Controls all else as with an iron rod ;
Like Joseph's sheaf, excelling all the rest,
They make obeisance to the bosom's god,
Which rules the mind with more despotic sway
Than Turkish Sultan or Morocco's Bey.

Each desire and passion but feeds this flame,
As lesser streams into the ocean flow,
Till glory, riches, reputation, fame
Are thrown aside, if by that fearful throw
We could attain, by this attain alone
A dream, perhaps—still what we doat upon.

Soon to our hero all nature wore
Another aspect; fields, flowers, streams and sky,
Were types of Heaven, seem'd to him far more
Than senseless things, for lovers' soul supply
The voids of nature, all must harmonize
With his imaginings, else the vision flies.

Love changes our being: the hue of human minds
Becomes celestial; love purifies
The dross of nature, and the lover finds
Delights in common place, his fancy flies
On wings seraphic, till what is human
Becomes angelic, and not a woman.

Alphonso was chang'd ere busy time had wrought
That change upon his face: such lines begin
When brows contract with contemplation, thought,
And furrows mar the beauty of the skin.
His face was calm, yet in his bosom swell'd
Intensest agony—a love withheld.

Oft was he known at even's quiet hour,
When loveless mortals are buried in repose,
Repair alone to grove or secret bower;
For crowds are solitude to him who knows
The ecstasies of love, a shooting star
Disturbs his soul as with a sudden jar.

His love was pure; aye such a love as spurns
The base alloy that mingles with the clod,
A spark akin to those that brightly burn
In hearts seraphic around the throne of God;
The hidden source, the golden tie that binds
In one, the earthly, with celestial minds.

But ah, how little a cold world can know
The deep emotions finer minds may feel,
The joy refin'd, the rapture, or the woe,
The thoughts of Heaven, that thro' its senses steal,
Yet know such thrills of joy intense or pain
Are deem'd as wand'rings of a mind insane.

Passions, contending elements that shake
The soul of genius, are eccentricities
To vulgar minds, whose vision cannot take
A deeper meaning than the multiplicities
Of outward seeming, measure all mankind
By compass meant but for a shallow mind.

Poor World! wretched, blind and piteous thing,
To patronize genius while genius holds
Humanity spell-bound, the only king
Of Spirit soul and mind, its spirit moulds
The destinies of nations: States may fall
And be forgotten; it survives thro' all.

Artists and poets lead two lives in one,
Two worlds are theirs—the one by right divine,
The other in common, neither can they shun
The carnal sense, altho' the spirit pine
In natures noble for the realms of art
For food to sate the hunger of the heart.

Ideals are perfect, the mind can frame
A Heav'n of its own, construct its hell,
The real tho' can never be the same,
Perfection never, purpos'd e'er so well
Attends the execution some fault will mar
The finest picture, dim the brightest star.

The maid Alphonso lov'd—who would not love
A maid so fair and beautiful as she?
All minds that have affinities above,
And must, per force, ne'er from its spell be free;
And altho' small the spark to mortals given,
'Tis all they know or ever feel of Heaven.

Alphonso's love was holy, pure and deep
As minds poetic never feign but feel,
A love remember'd even in his sleep,
Which in sweet dreams did o'er his senses steal,.
An impress leaving upon unconscious hours
As dews from Heaven refresh the faded flowers.

No man walks the earth in solitude,
For solitude is yet a thing unknown,
Except in name; for spirits, ill or good,
Are with us in crowds or when we seem alone.
Tho' they be hid thro' life from sensual view,
Are there not times when they can speak to you?'

But love alone, for mere created good
Deprives the soul of power to attain
This higher sphere and causes it to brood
O'er fancied ills and self-inflicted pain,
Or cheats itself with sensual delights,
Till woman bounds the limit of its flights.

Ah, had he ne'er from such sweet dreams awoke;.
It had been well and he had never borne
The load of sorrow, or with torture broke
Upon the wheel of fate, nor inly torn
By the heart's dread demon—a fell despair,
Which only feels a spirit doom'd to bear.

Sweet vision of bliss, of sublunary bliss,
How trusting hearts become an easy prey
To thy sweet flatteries in a world like this,
Where naught is sweet save what our souls convey
From self-built heavens to slake immortal thirst,
And hunger for fruits sin hath not marr'd nor curst..

ALPHONSO.

But bound in Love's elysian bands he lay
A willing captive, thinking he was free,
While ev'ry fetter tightened day by day
With that delusion love alone can see.
Yet lovers' hopes can swim upon a straw,
And love can see what reason never saw.

Perhaps the pangs the spirit torn endures
In such a state is harder to be borne
Than pure despair, the antidote that cures
The sore from which the bandage should be torn ;
Love, to be heal'd, must have a cruel nurse,
Sympathy only makes the patient worse.

Love must be met with love, one cannot quench
Longings insatiate with sympathy alone ;
Better the flower we sever at a wrench
Than pluck it by piecemeal till it be gone,
'Tis death by subtraction, an instant blow
Is far more merciful, it ends all woe.

But deeply, purely as our hero lov'd,
His was a common fate, he lov'd in vain.
By love the least a woman's heart is moved,
Love gains the least what it is wont to gain,
A mad conceit, oh wild impetuous heart,
To think that woman is won except by art.

A woman true is Heaven's richest gift,
A woman false a ruin and a curse,
The first can elevate our souls and lift
Our minds above a darkened universe,
Up to the throne and bright abode of Him,
Around whom dwell the glowing seraphim.

The darkest story a lunatic can tell,
Is a blighted love, yet all may not be told
Unless our eyes could see each secret hell
Consuming hearts, the dross as well as gold,
How woman false can rivet, chain and bind,
And poison the fountains of a feeling mind.

The deepest minds are those that suffer most,
The shallow one, not dignified with sorrow ;
The one allied to a celestial host,
The other earthy, cannot lend nor borrow,
Poverty wretched, of life as well as thought,
Ciphers on life's state standing there for naught.

There does exist in mind, as well as matter
Abhorence of nothingness ; so we create
Where naught exists, and endow the latter
With functions spiritual, this boon hath fate
Vouchsafed to minds creative, sea, earth and sky,
Are more than matter to a poet's eye.

The mind therefore that sorrow does not sway,
Nor love excite, nor fame enchant at least,
Is hardly more, nor scarcely less than clay
Impress'd by forms methodically pieced,
And put together, lacking all essentials
Entitling man to divine credentials.

Alphonso's hour had come, the hour when he
Should speak to one the pathos of his heart,
When he should seek an humble an humble devotee,
Devoid of no feeling the immortal part
Of man's nature cannot feign but feel,
When brought so near to future wo or weal.

But our hero like to some artless child
With the knife of fate in his skillless hands
Impetuous, excitable and wild,
Gashes himself, and sees the silken strands
Of hope asunder part, and this is life
To stab our own hearts with a borrow'd knife.

Alphonso fail'd, the maiden was unmoved
By all that beam'd from his pleading eyes,
By time alone to eager hearts is proved,
How vain are all our tenderness and sighs,
Unless our idol in our feelings share,
And in our love, a due proportion bear.

No life is perfect that has not met deceit,
And more is woman lov'd as she betrays
And her sweet falsities have power to cheat
The heart of man, still Delilah's now-adays
Yet swindle man's love : Eve, the first and best,
Frail as she was, but typifies the rest.

And whom does woman love ? Let those decide
Whom stern experience surely guides aright,
The flashy rake with all things else denied
Except a tongue, he is the depth and height
Of her imaginings of an ideal man,
This may be slander ; deny it if you can.

This is the usual woman, there are of course
Exceptions ever to a general rule,
Such rules us'd only as a last resource
When press'd in argument, and yet a fool
May wed a woman of as good a kind
As the rugg'd giant in the world of mind.

But Love—the heaven of the youthful heart,
The source of sweets, Thee must we deify
In spite of common sense, and play our part
In that wild romance where tear and sigh
And smile are magnified and made to mean
Indices of destiny in some trivial scene.

Love unrequited, bitter are thy pangs
To youthful hearts, and wrenching at a blow
The fairest flower, and in a moment bangs
The door of fate in face of all below,
Deem'd earthly happiness, bitter fate indeed
To one who sees young joy's dream recede.

Ah, then the forms seem vile of this fair world,
Save Natures only and a living ray
Illumines the inanimate, with forms unfurled
Doth Beauty beam, where once but darkless lay,
Yet doom'd by fate most cruel and unkind,
The soul still starves for love it cannot find.

Yet in all Natures' multifarious forms
No voice ministers to the soul of man
Like hers we love, the crash of storms,
The zephyr's sigh, in turn may serve to fan
Poetic fire, yet cannot be a cure
For wounds that wretched hearts alone endure.

Alphonso's soul became a ceaseless prey
To melancholy, every bird that sung,
Seem'd chanting a requiem of hope's burial day,
For but one hope had cheer'd his heart when young:
And that was gone, a dark and dreamless void,
With naught save memory of a love destroyed.

The saddest sight to see another's joy
When we are wretched, contrast digs a hell
That awes the devil, and laughter can destroy
A man's philosophy, for who can quell
The demon within us, put to open shame
By heartless mirth or real, all the same.

But why repine, the universal soul
Of Nature only bids man rejoice,
If in his gay moments, her charms cajole
And for his sad ones, a sympathising voice,
It shows a heart untrue, a will perverse,
Not to be sooth'd by such a genial nurse.

Then after all, perhaps for whom you sigh
Sighs for another who does not love her more
Than she does you, and who could not deny
Himself of bliss in order to secure
A lov'd one's happiness, but no one can,
Unless an Angel, never selfish man.

But ah! too deeply had Alphonso loved
And too unselfishly, no single blow
Can sever hearts, that spell must be removed
By time and distance, till the long ago
Looms up once more, a heaven—not a hell
And experience tells us that it ended well.

Yet strange indeed that ever man should yearn
And sigh for her whose sighs are not for him,
That he will from each pleasing prospect turn
To gaze on pictures feelingless and dim,
Nor snap at once the smallest thread that binds
The corpse that fate hath fasten'd our minds.

More foolish still that brilliant minds are wasted
In efforts fruitless to win an icy heart,
'Twere better far love's sweetness were untasted,
Than for it lose existence' better part;
For, after all, 'tis but a dubious chase,
Where oft times worst is he who wins the race.

And yet despair, ah who can better know it
Than he alone, whom fate hath made to feel;
Untold by all the frenzies of the poet,
Language is impotent its horrors to reveal,
And so to shun and feel that we are free,
We cling to hope and will not let her flee.

Of all the strange delusions of our youth
This is perhaps the strangest of them all:
That we will shut our eyes against the truth,
As if afraid that truth would ruin all,
And nurse love lost as children would a sore,
Which, to be heal'd, needs but neglect—no more.

This truth at last flash'd o'er Alphonso's mind,
And, strange to him, it made his heart serene,
And made him seek, by leaving hope behind,
Another joy amid a change of scene;
Yet, ere he left, his soul was wont to pour
This plaintive lay to all he lov'd before:

    " 'Tis sad to know when I am gone
       Thou'lt cease to think of me,
    Of one whose heart was all thine own,
       His dearest thought for thee.

    But when thy heart and hand shall be
       For one who loves thee less,
    Let not one painful thought of me
       E'er pain thee or distress.

Tho' to a bleak and barren world
    I turn with aching heart,
With all my heaven in chaos hurl'd
    And pierced with sorrows dart.

Be thou the joyous maiden still
    Thou wert in hours past,
My anguish time at length must kill,
    Love but with hope can last.

Tho' for thy love I would have given
    This dreary world beside,
My sweetest thought this side of Heaven
    That you would be my bride.

'Twas not thy fault thou could'st not feel
    All I have felt for thee,
But mine to mourn a baffled zeal,
    For hopes unkind to me.

Amid a cheerless world shall I
    Be fated yet to find
That love that beams from woman's eye
    To soothe a darken'd mind."

CANTO II.

The love of life is one of nature's laws,
The fear of death a counterpart to this,
Which seems to be an intervening clause
In every way man hath of earthly bliss;
For pleasure and pain, nay e'en death and life
Are terms convertible, so are peace and strife.

B

And what is life?   At best to all, not some,
A few brief years the circle must complete,
When the warm heart must wither and become
Food for the worms that crawl beneath our feet,
And this is life, at least the common lot,
To breathe, to die, and then to be forgot.

Yet some, in one, may live out many lives,
Each part of which would make another's whole
They are, to whom, both God and Nature give
So much of heart, of sentiment and soul,
Who feel far more, no doubt, within a year
Than others do throughout a life's career.

And such are they who win a deathless name
Yet fail to win what they so madly sought,
One object loved, and what solace hath fame
Unshared by those so dear to ev'ry thought?
None that we know of save the innate pride
That we achieve that for which millions died.

In proof of this immortal Petrarch lives
Along with Laura, while Byron brightly shines
And dazzles Mary with the light he gives
From his own great soul that beams in all his lines.
Ah, rustic maid, the charms of brawny youth
Were more to thee than mightiest fame forsooth.
      *   *   *   *   *   *   *

Our hero again upon the scene appears;
But ah, how changed to him the hues of life!
Scorch'd with siroccos and burning tears;
Its flowers faded, once with beauty rife,
All earth a desert, a rude and barren waste
And peopled with phantoms, once for substance chased—

The pangs of disappointed love no more
Did pain his heart, altho' its stings were there,
For passion's power and ecstasy were o'er
Since heavenly hope had yielded to despair;
And now his mind, like some mad meteor hurled,
Ran lawless thro' an intellectual world.

The long exploded systems of the past,
The boast dogmas of the present day,
Served but to give his hungry mind repast,
To be enjoyed, then vilely thrown away,
A skeptic more by impulse than by reason,
A heart that fear'd but one thing—that was treason.

A mental miser he at length became,
And hoarded learning, alone for learning's sake;
Aiming, aiming ever, and yet without an aim,
Careless what course his destiny should take,
The life he led contain'd no charm or sweet:
Existence merely—a chain he must complete.

There are strokes that scorch the soul and sear
The very heart, as lightning doth the tree,
Depriving its buds the power to appear,
Much less to bloom where they were wont to be.
'Tis thus affections, wither'd at a blow,
Decay in hearts where they were wont to glow.

The mind of man may still expand, create,
New worlds of thought and systems of its own
E'en while his heart cannot reciprocate
These high delights, its one enjoyment gone,
Can find none other, tho' others could be found
As sweet as this would he but look around.

When passion's storm hath spent itself in vain,
And coldness meets its elements of fire,
Like barren wastes that drink the genial rain,
And yield no fruit, except the thorn and briar,
The mind recoils upon itself to feel
The sharpest pangs of its unpitied zeal.

The heart recedes, the mind again appears
To body forth scenes of sublimer beauty,
Music mysterious in nature hears,
The full force feels, of doing ev'ry duty
Despite life's petty ills, subdued by sorrow,
Strong to prevail o'er what may come to-morrow.

A world of beauty, despite what cynics' say;
Aye, worthy Him who made and form'd it all,
Creation's lamp, the glorious orb of day,
The moon that beams when shades nocturnal fall,
The starry host.   Who is not made to feel
A sense of beauty o'er his spirit steal?

Moments there are, when mortals seem to stand
Upon the line, the measureless frontier,
Which bars the earthly from celestial land:
Our spirits there, alas our bodies here!
But ah, too soon, does passion bubble up
And senses spoil the nectar in our cup.

And it was thus Alphonso's mind became
A part and parcel of all that met its gaze,
Objects inanimate, with phantasy and flame,
His soul imbued; not passions sickly blaze,
The song of birds, the gurgling of the stream
More potent to move than was Love's early dream.

And what is poetry? Easier asked than told,
A few indeed have its spirit known.
Some deem it an impulse all uncontrolled,
The truth of which remaineth to be shown.
Like other gifts of a celestial source,
A mortal pride must claim it all of course.

All men are poets, indeed there are but few
Who have not felt at times and own'd its flame.
A difference slight exists between the two,
Thought may be strong while language may be lame;
For natures e'en impassive as a stone
Have surely once some genuine impulse known.

The poet's heart is but a pit of flame,
Like Etna's bosom, boiling when at rest,
His object never to win a deathless name,
But vent in song what pains him when suppressed,
Purg'd by the fires that in his bosom prey
E'en common-place then ceases to be clay.

And in such moments when the cup of life
Seems o'er running with delicious nectar,
Then is the soul of poesy all rife
With beauteous forms of ev'ry mental spectre,
Aye nymph and sprite adorn the mental scene,
And sport and gambol on Fancy's fairy green.

'Tis then with all her pencillings of flame
She adds new beauties to each scene of bliss,
And paints so fair her ideal world 'twould shame
One dwelling there to say he came from this.
Thus minds can make a heaven of their own
And diamonds fashion from mud and stone.

But this alone is not her fav'rite field,
She dwells within, as well as flies amain,
And tho' to her the vulgar heart be steel'd,
Yet she will rise superior to her pain,
From gloomy cell or closely guarded prison,
Earth-shaking speech, to Heaven hath arisen.

But genius still may have its kindlings crushed
By sheer neglect, or bitter, cold disdain,
But never yet hath man thy spirit hushed,
Powerless he, its rapture to restrain,
And thus adown the avenues of time,
Its spirit speaks in prose, or blazing rhyme.

No, none can prison the spirits mighty dream,
Altho' unseen, unread by mortal eye,
For it can mingle with the rushing stream,
And blend with all beauty in earth or sky,
Contriving ever 'mid outward forms to find
The beauty lost upon the vulgar mind.

And yet withal may poesy still cope
With all the passions of the human heart,
All hues of joy, the rainbow tints of hope,
And then despair, when hope and joy depart,
All power to pierce the densities of life
And see the pearls beneath the streams of strife.

In ev'ry age her votaries have found
A fabric this on which to rear their fame,
For there are thoughts, which in the soul abound,
Which all may feel and yet but few can name,
The poet then, but tells what all may feel,
He must speak out: No poet can conceal.

To some is given sublimity and power,
With tireless wing to soar the heights of song,
To paint the lightning when the tempests lower,
Or join the thunder in its mountain song,
To seize the strains immense, that ocean sings,
And know their meaning ; these are spirit-kings.

Of such is he, who feels celestial fire,
Which but in hearts of higher nature glows,
And from his soul, a heav'n accorded lyre,
Come forth such strains, as but his spirit knows.
On time's threshold, his province is to stand
To echo back strains from immortal strand.

   * * * * * * *

There is commingled in the cup of being
An equal mixture of bitterness and bliss,
For Beauty's self would pall upon the seeing,
Were there no contrast found on earth to this.
The tempest that bends the sturdy oak to earth,
The lurid lightning and the roaring thunder,
Were better than dull monotony or dearth
Of aught that may excite our minds to wonder,
Yet who could wish that lovely Natures' face
Should frown for aye, nor cheer us with a smile?
Each season serves in its appointed place,
And hath its charms existence to beguile,
Nor do we lose 'mid Spring of light and mirth,
The joys of Winter around the blazing hearth—

It is the poet's privilege to bring
All scenes of life before the mental view,
And his own heart, (if he has such a thing,)
Must oft be wrung, that he may sing for you.
What are deep feelings but the wells of life,
Supplying those whose nature cannot know

What beauties spring from intellectual strife,
What precious drops are wrung from mortal woe!
For words, no ray of feelings permeate,
Of lifeless things, are most inanimate.

Yet some contend that music is the source
Whence liquid numbers of the poet flow,
Others say "Love," and love of course,
No minor part can act in scenes below.
These may excite, (the germ is in the soul)
The plant to grow, until it doth attain
A height to Heav'n—its tendrils all unroll—
Its flowers fall on mountain top and plain,
For the divine of all poetic art,
Is that which stays the hunger of the heart.

Thus thought Alphonso, for such thoughts did give
His spirit ease or transitory joy;
A life most loath'd hath aught to make us live
One bliss perchance, that nothing can destroy.
The veriest wretch, in all his rags and dirt,
A joy nurses that time hath never hurt.

But Nature's forms lead up to Nature's God
The spirit thoughtful, seeking thus to find
That haven of hearts once smitten by the rod
Of fate most merciless, and the darken'd mind
Sees light break thro' the bosom of the cloud
And hears the small voice that speaks to it aloud.

To our hero mountains and stars became
The syllables of life, from which e'er long he learned
To spell man's destiny e'er his heart could frame
The wondrous thought for which his spirit yearned,
Holiness, by which, (so says the written word)
None may see God, the once Incarnate Lord.

No mind is noble which does not sigh for this,
No heart is pure whose best emotions rise
Beneath this thought, the one supremest bliss
To be conceiv'd by mortal 'neath the skies.
Such thought best shows, no other proof be given,
Man is immortal, his lineage sprung in Heav'n.

Holiness only, since the fall of man,
Has puzzled hell, Satannic intellect
Is all eclips'd, and can conceive no plan
To thwart its force, no cunning to detect
A single flaw in what was seen and known
In Mind Almighty, aye in God alone.

To know of this, not that forbidden tree
Which grew in Eden, Alphonso pray'd and sighed,
And sought in books: these seldom leave us free
From their misgivings, an uncertain guide
That leads in paths where others have been lost,
A bark in seas of speculation tost.

For him the face of Nature wore all moods,
Yet without charms, as when in musing hour,
He sought the field or wander'd through the woods,
Where dulcet notes rang out from branch and bower,
For this, alas not God's appointed plan
To bring relief or soothe the soul of man.

Alphonso was not happy, still his mind
Would yet revert and conjure back the past
With life's first joy that time had left behind
E'er blown upon by Hate's siroccoed blast.
A change of heart, as well as mind must be
E'er man can take his place among the free.

'Twas vain he sought a solace for his soul
'Mid woods and rocks, or solitary vale,
Tho' for the mind may Nature's stores unroll,
Within the heart will sorrow still prevail,
So with our hero, who in strains like these
Pour'd forth his soul alone to give it ease.

" My breast is rack'd with many a pang,
   More keen than poet ever sang,
   Nor can it till compos'd of steel,
   E'er feign a joy it cannot feel.
   The leafless tree, the riven oak,
   Once blasted by the lightning's stroke.
   Might sooner hope to bud again,
   Than my poor heart forget its pain,
   For within it I feel a void
   Of ev'ry hope that once employed
   And yet in vain I strive for more
   Than what the vulgar herd adore.
   And yet, alas! what boots that I
   Should strive for excellence or sigh
   For what is noble; am I not
   'Mid thoughtless throngs obscured, forgot,
   My flowers trampled in the dust,
   My gems consign'd away to rust,
   My precious thoughts, my golden rules
   Become the laughing-stock of fools?
   Still in imaginative flight
   My mind shall soar the dizzy height,
   Then look beneath, through fancy's glass,
   In scorn upon the vulgar mass,
   Who scoff because I deign to soar
   Beyond the heights their minds explore.
   Alas! that on this icy steep
   Where thought alone may deign to sweep,
   No flowers bloom, no linnets sing,

No warm, reviving breath of Spring,
No sympathetic heart to share
Our gloomy grandeur or despair.
Tho' higher natures love to stray
'Mid blazing stars, or milky-way,
Tho' Genius in its flight can bear
Our spirits from the spheres that are
To others built of bright romance,
Where all things seem but to enhance
Our high delights, an earthly tie
Contrives to drag us from the sky;
For without this would genius be
Beyond thy pale, Mortality!
Nor can all fame or glory give
That which makes our bliss to live,
Nor mid its glare can we forget
One star of hope that may have set
In early life to which we gave,
Our very being as a slave.
Tho' much mine erring mind hath stray'd
Thro' light and darkness, shine and shade,
Tho' much I've striven to forget
My heart, my HEART, is lonely yet."

CANTO III.

Misguided man, who seeks ethereal bliss,
Save in communion, with his Maker, God,
Wanders but blindly from the path of peace,
Nor e'er returns, till the chast'ning rod,
Of sore affliction bid his spirit seek
The Rock of Ages—Tower of the weak.

For tho' the mountain and old ocean tell
In eloquence mute, of Him who made them all,
They tell not man, how he from Eden fell,
Nor curse attending his nature from the fall,

Nor e'er yet was man so wise as find
In nature's book, his dread Creator's mind.

*   *   *   *   *   *   *

The morn was calm, as morns may be in June,
And birds sung out from ev'ry branch and bower,
And man's dark spirit could mingle and commune
With Nature's beauty till the silent power,
Of thought's transfusion, made it all his own,
Alphonso, (as wont) his morning ramble took
Along the vale, and by the babbling brook.

Till lost in thought at length, he sat him down
Beneath the shade of an outspreading oak,
To muse on man, the hero, king and clown,
Then of himself, who groan'd beneath the yoke,
Of one misfortune, aye, that one is sooth,
Which erst had crush'd the joys of his youth.

The mem'ry of one, whose sweet and guileless face
Had been his youth's heaven, did meet him there
In all its beauty, winsomeness and grace,
With her dark eyes beaming, and her silken hair
Of auburn beauty, wreath'd yet with flowers
Himself had pluck'd for her in happier hours.

The same sweet smile, which once had won its way
To his once young heart, he beheld again,
Yet, not as then, he yielded to its sway,
For it was steel'd by agony and pain,
Which mean experience, taught him now to shun,
Or be suspicious of all he looked upon.

Just then a sound borne softly thro' the air,
Dissolv'd the spell which was around him thrown,
A sound that call'd to penitence and prayer,
A Sabbath bell, whose sweetly solemn tone

Seem'd apropos to that sad train of thought
With which his heart and mind alike were fraught.

Yet, e're he left the consecrated spot,
While his soul was kindled with poetic fire,
To her, not then, nor now, nor e'er forgot
He struck this music from his spirits' lyre.

"REMEMBRANCE."

"Sweet Lady, believe me, time cannot destroy,
   Thine image of beauty on my soul deeply wrought,
But still it remaineth diffusing its joy,
   On the track of each bodiless thought.

Long since have I ceas'd both to sigh and repine,
   For a love, which you cannot return,
But alas, when I look at that dear face of thine,
   Love still in my bosom will burn.

Tho' my beautiful Eden is denied me by fate,
   And bade me its pleasures to sever,
There's a measure of bliss could I stand at the gate
   And gaze on its beauties forever.

When my last sands of life shall be ebbing forever,
   May thine image, sweet Lady, to my spirit be given,
That its last glimpse of beauty, as it passes the river
   Shall be kindred to that which shall meet it in Heaven."

An humble fane, that pious hands had reared,
Stood in a grove, hard by Alphonso's oak,
From which came forth the sounds he lately heard,
And which unwitting, his reverie had broke,
He listen'd and heard in measur'd cadence roll
Hymns sweet because the language of the soul.
  C

And ceasing this, he heard the voice of prayer,
No solemn mouthing, sanctimonious phrase,
Instructing God to witness and compare
Their saintly lives, with such as spend their days
In sins rebellious, not this our hero heard,
But God's own promise in his written word.

Strange, yet true, that trifles in themselves
Are oft precursors to results as great
As any found by him who toils and delves
In the deep mines of thought to expurgate,
By rugged logic and argument, forsooth,
The dross of error from the gem of truth.

The warm, untutor'd language of the heart
Deals unbelief a more disastrous blow
Than weighty words of controversial art,
Wherewith men strive to prove a God or no,
That proof at best lies hidden in the heart,
And trifles make it into action start.

He whom the voice of Nature had not taught
The way of life, nor theologian wise,
The utmost limits of permitted thought,
Now found it in forests, where prayer could rise,
From hearts untaught, except that God is good ;
This is enough to save a world, and should.

Alphonso like, the wearied dove of old,
Had found no rest, and so had sought in vain
Thro' many creeds, in which he had been told
Were antidotes for all of earthly pain,
But found as others, who seek in stalls and shelves,
Books mostly plead the merit of themselves.

The Spirit's sword soon pierced him to the heart,
And God's own truth was fasten'd in his mind;
Still man may shun e'en Heaven's appointed dart,
And force his way to hell, perverse and blind,
Lose endless life, lose Heaven, all things, and choose
Eternal torments than life's pleasures lose.

Not so with him who both had seen and tasted
The best and worst that is to mortal given,
Nor one who felt life's sweetest prospect wasted,
For him to seek 'mid ceaseless pain his heaven,
Nor vent his soul in misanthropic spite,   .
While realms remain, where all is love and light.

And ere the sun that late in beauty rose,
Had sought its couch, the bosom of the deep,
Did love divine, like that a seraph knows
Shine in his soul and made his spirit leap
From dark misgivings, oh, glorious thought!
To certain hope, and God the change had wrought.

He is free alone, whom the Word makes free,
God by wisdom to man may not be known;
Nor all thy systems, proud Philosophy,
The path to bliss to him hath never shown,
But endless maze, in speculation lost,
Until the line that bounds our fate is crossed.

But what is true worship? Does it depend
On attitude or else some form or rite,
Whereby the knee of man is made to bend,
His eye upturn, each act devout, contrite?
Ah, no, the prayer that best ascends to Heaven,
Is that to which no utterance can be given.

The thirst and hunger of the human heart
For what is good or beautiful or true;
Purging man's nature from its baser part;
Filling his soul to act as angels' do,
Union mysterious with God's Anointed Son,
In Heaven completed, yet on earth begun,—

No human weakness can impair its strength,
'Tis built on God and he upholds it all,
The sceptic's sneer to horror turns at length,
The jesting scoffer reads upon the wall
His fearful doom, "I am the Way, the Truth,
Co-equal with God,"—his very Son forsooth.

It was thus our hero felt and thought,
Despite what those who wed to form might say;
Again his heart, by deeper feeling wrought,
Essay'd to sing this bold yet humble lay:

"TRUTH."

"If the doctrine be true, which the orthodox hold,
That sin is pernicious to the life of the soul,
Then truly the pathway of life is all hidden,
Since the spirit still craves what it feels is forbidden,
Great God of all Truth from blindness relieve me,
From creeds and confessions that may but deceive me,—
Thou hast left me the volume of Nature to scan,
And the Book of all Truth, not the doctrines of man,
These taught me the only true pathway to bliss
Was acceptance of that or rejection of this,
Made me to believe that what I had done
More precious to thee than the blood of thy Son.
'Tis a proneness of all in the weakness of youth
To believe all the errors that are taught them for truth,
Thou hast given to mortals no power to bind

Or shackle thine image, the fetterless mind,
Thou dwellest in temples not made with the hand,
But alone in the sanctified spirit of man,
Forgiving all deeds we have wickedly done
And making us stainless in the blood of thy Son,
I feel all the service thou demandest of me,
Is to worship in spirit, which is kindred to thee.
The day is not distant in which he shall tremble
Once wont in thy presence to cloak and dissemble,
The short-sighted creatures who strove to conceal
Their rottenness moral by a show of false zeal,
That glance in moment sees eternity through,
Be certain, oh false one, ever looking on you,
From deception, hypocrisy and the nature sin gave me,
I beseech thee, Oh Father, to snatch me and save me,
Preserve me, sustain me, and appoint me to stand,
At the Day of all days upon thy right hand."

Alas! in this enlightened day of ours
Too many yet to senseless forms are wed,
Forms are but weeds that choke life's fairest flowers,
And yield no fruit but briars in their stead.
If man must wrangle, why not wrangle more
For truth than robes that Paul or Peter wore?

No one is free, for doubts alike will prey,
Like gnawing worms, at any root of faith,
Which some mistake for holiness, decay,
To pressure yield and then are swept beneath;
Approach the city until its gates are seen,
Then backward turn if doubts but intervene.

The man of God must ever be prepared,
And o'er himself incessant vigils keep,
Hug no delusion, tho' by millions shared,
A shepherd knowing aright to guide his sheep.
The mind, once bound in superstitious bands,
Is like an infant in a giant's hands.

CANTO IV.

It is not good that man should be alone,
Almighty Wisdom, when he made him said,
And eras present, and all the ages gone
Attest this truth, in the beginning said:
For since *Pere* Adam took Mother Eve to wife,
'Tis implied censure to lead a single life.

Man left alone is far more desolate
Than even woman ; she contrives to find
Some good excuse for such a loveless fate,
She could not see one suited to her mind ;
He saw a dozen, mayhap lost them all
By leaving till Spring the event of the Fall.

Books, friends, for a season may beguile his heart,
And cheat it a moment to forget its sorrow,
But bliss attends no servile trains of art,
Man's mind or heart no outward ease can borrow,
But in itself alone can hope to find
The image pleasing that soothes a darken'd mind

Still man may live all reasonably well,
Until at length the ideal hour is past,
When sighs have ceased to own some silly belle,
And real woman asserts her sway at last,
And when, too late, the tables may be turned
And he loses rightly what he may have spurned.

Creation's lords, at best, are but a part
Of a common unit much as they may swell
Out of proportion : this is only art ;
Woman knows this, indeed she knows it well,
And can contrive some way to coax and cozen
And gull your lords by units of a dozen.

The lilly pale that blooms in lone retreat
Soon fades away in short-lived beauty there ;
Denied the dew, the fructifying heat,
Breathing from birth a pestilential air,
So human hearts, denied the light of love,
Lose that existence God gives them from above.

More so, when one hath pour'd his soul in vain,
As water lavished on the fruitless sand,
And thorns alone are products of his pain,
Or nettles thrive where flowers hop'd to stand,
Each heart requires some feeling soul to share :
Pain loses weight when there are two to bear.

Yet after Love, one thing remains to stir
The human heart, man's own created god,
Ambition—dreams that high-born minds prefer
To vulgar pleasures of the senseless clod.
And this belongs to that imperial few
Whose darkest deeds seem grandly glorious too.

But let not him, of all, presume to judge,
By his own gauge, who ne'er goes beyond
The dusty roads, where sweating millions trudge,
Nor envy him, whose mind and heart hath spurn'd,
All vulgar things, for some are born to sway,
While others rise by learning to obey.

This prompting too may be no base desire ;
No sinful motion of a wicked heart ;
No carnal passion, no unhallow'd fire ;
But that which moves to take a higher part,
In life's endeavor, than listlessly to wait,
And catch at straws, or else be drown'd by fate.

But to its own, where it of right should be,
The mind will tend, and there delighted dwell,
In its element only is genius free,
All others are prisons or a loathesome cell,
Where all deprived the power of its wings,
It loathes, not loves, the sight of vulgar things;.
And thus Alphonso, chafing with desire,
Enslaved by want and visited with wrong
From many a source, again took up his lyre
And pour'd again his sadden'd soul in song:—

"OBLIVION."

"Am I, beneath the lonely mound,
To moulder nameless in the ground,
Nor let a record here remain
That I have liv'd altho' in vain
Nor carry to my dreamless bed,
No form on which my fancy fed?
Shall all the hopes of former years,
Joys that shone thro' sorrow's tears,—
Shall love, celestial in its source,
Acknowledge death's relentless force;
Shall hope recede, be felt no more,
When once the fitful dream is o'er?
Or shall the senseless clods that fall
Upon my coffin bury all?
Tho' flowers bloom upon my grave,
And bending cypress gently wave,
Whose pendant branches swept by air
A ceaseless requiem sing me there;
Or little bird within the bower,
Above me sing at even's hour,
Yet who would deign a tear to shed
Above the soon forgotten dead,
Rememb'ring naught that he hath said
Or done for good of human kind;

Aye, to a common lot consigned,
Forgotten, dead, and out of mind?
Altho' my soul I feel to be
A spark of immortality,
Fain would I live when I am dead,
In deeds or words that I have said.
An honor to my race and name,
The parent stock from whence I came,
Like Scotia's Burns with magic art
To stir the fountains of the heart,
Or Byron, whose imperial soul
Broke thro' all fetters and control.
Oblivion, oh thy dreadful name,
Whose waters quench the spirit's flame,
That word can dig a deeper hell
Than even wrath divine would tell.
E'en here thy horrors seem to chill,
The spark that ocean's cannot kill;
Sulphureous horrors milder seem
Than such as hang o'er Lethe's stream.
Oh, Soul! arise, assert, and claim
Thine inheritance of fame;
Breathe forth the fires in thy breast,
In lurid flame, if suit thee best,
Or pour thy numbers as the shower
That beautifies the field and flower;
Or vent perchance the bosom's spleen,
In satire edg'd, sharp and keen,
All things, save to dullness wed,
To sink among the nameless dead."

There is nothing so wounding to a woman's pride,
As thoughts of yielding her love unsought;
And yet all other, tho' it be denied,
Deserves not the name—love is not bought;
Nor fashion'd in beauty as a thing of art,
But beautiful only when it owns the heart.

Love is not voluntary; 'tis a fall,
Or the soul uplifted by a secret power;
A love explain'd is no love at all,
Rob it of mystery it does not live an hour.
Love, Genius and Madness are near the same,
The mind on fire, the heart a pit of flame.

And Friendship and Love no relation bear
Or near connection as the vale and hill,
For cannot lovers even malice bear;
Aye, hate each other, and be lovers still?
And whereas Doubt is ever Friendship's knell,
'Tis true love's proof—(fond lover mark it well.)

Our knowledge most from contrast is derived,
Who, with all day, would ever darkness know;
So love forever, of a doubt deprived,
Soon loses force: 'tis doubt that makes it so:
For doubt is but twin-sister of desire,
The fuel that feeds our faith's refining fire.

'Twixt hate and love is but a step between,
Or rather in essence they are the same,
Like the viewless borders which intervene
'Twixt light and darkness, when the dying flame
Of day departing, mingles into night,
Till the line is lost, dividing dark and light.

A maiden lovely in spirit as in form,
A Star of Beauty with no borrow'd light,
Arose at length and bade at once the storm
Be past which preyed upon our hero's sight.
With her he wed, liv'd happy with his bride,
Were lov'd by all—lamented when they died.

EUREKA.

TO MY FRIENDS, THOMAS W. TIMBERLAKE AND LADY.

EXORDIUM.

While others sing of Grecian Isles,
In strains that ev'ry heart beguiles,
How warriors fought and cities fell
For Helen, false and fickle belle;
How Miltiade's army stood
A bulwark to the Persian flood,
And roll'd it backward, as the tide,
That madly smites the mountain's side,
Let sterner mind its thought employ,
With Marathon or burning Troy;
Let these and mightier themes belong
To Homers of immortal song;
Let Miltons with angelic eye,
Behold the battles of the sky,
Or turn with equal sweep and tell
The secrets of the lowest hell;
Let Swifts and Butlers ridicule
The knave and Puritanic school;
Let Byrons in the realms of rhyme
Make darkness light and lust sublime;
Mine be the sweeter task to trace
The giant footsteps of the race,
And sing in unmistaken tone
Of great creations, not my own.
I to others leave the task
Vice to denounce: I only ask
The God of Song that he imbue

My spirit with the good and true;
To open up a brighter way,
That leads from darkness into day, ·
To break the fetters that control
The life and freedom of the soul,
This be the noble aim to-day
That prompts me to this crude essay.

EUREKA.

I.

In days remote there dwelt amain,
A mortal deem'd by some insane;
A man from lowly parents sprung,
To whom no titles did belong,
Whose youth was spent, as he was poor,
In driving famine from his door,
No events mark'd his early years,
Except the sports which youth reveres;
No meteor shot athwart his sky,
To pall his sense or dim his eye;
Yet in his soul there dwelt a fire,
Unquench'd by lust or low desire,
Which mov'd his mind to enterprise
By paths unseen to others' eyes.
The giddy throng that moves below
Such mines of thought can never know,
But is content to live and dwell
Around the door of wisdom's cell.
It sees, alas! but darkness there,
Where dwell the stores of beauty rare.
The gems of truth that brightly shine,
And beckon on with light divine,
Are but as pearl before the swine;
And truths' wrench'd up from error's main,
By busy thought and aching brain,

By efforts of the mightiest mind,
Are thrown as chaff before the wind.
Not thus the man of other days,
With spirit kindled at the blaze
Of inspiration sent from Him,
Who made the glowing Cherubim.

*   *   *   *   *   *   *

The merest trifle often brings
A glimpse of most surprising things,
And truths and facts of wondrous worth
To them alone oft owe their birth.
An apple falling to the ground
Prov'd all things to one centre bound;
A kettle boiling on the fire,
Which shook the lid as if with ire,
Prov'd what had been before a dream,
The strength and majesty of steam.
No flight of fancy could have told
How planets in their orbits roll'd;
No madman's brain, however great,
Could e'er have found such strength in heat;
There must be long, laborious thought,
When once the chain is fairly caught,
And link by link severely wrought,
To forge the links of evidence,
Beyond the ken of common sense.
The powers of the master mind
Shirks not the labor of this kind.
Perceptive powers made to pierce
The secrets of the Universe,
In trifles small obtain the key
To all of Nature's mystery,
That opes creation's vaults to see,
The hidden wealth of mind and thought,
Where dunces quake and see but naught.
Nature crowns such sons of hers
    D

Her genuine interpreters,
And these are they whom God consigns
To manifest the light that shines
O'er all his works, and roll away
The stone where buried wisdom lay ;
For every twig, and leaf, and flower,
Are tokens of design and power ;
Aye, ev'ry blade of grass that grows,
Examin'd well, some knowledge shows.
The veriest insect that can crawl,
Tho' infintessimally small
To human optics, yet portrays
That Wisdom rules in all his ways.
The varied faculties of man
Were given him to probe and scan,
With reason giv'n to deduce
Their sev'ral purposes and use.
'Twas thus the mighty Newton told
How planets in their orbits roll'd ;
By this a Fulton learn'd to team
A vessel drawn by steeds of steam ;
Thus Franklin, with his paper kite,
Disgorg'd the clouds' electric light,
And gave to Morse, by more than half,
His idea of the telegraph.
The idea first on Nature's page
Is seen by philosophic sage,
Theory next is brought to view,
Then practice comes, and all is true.
What gives to some such mental power
To pierce the mists that 'round them lower ?
Is Being's scale exalted so,
That few may rise where others go ?
It is because we shrink from thought,
In seeing Nature as we ought;
Or, with that tameness which subdues,

What reason and what judgment choose,
With soul and mind to dullness wed
We sink among the nameless dead.
Not thus the man of olden time,
With spirit full of thought sublime,
By deep research and reason clear
Had found the earth indeed a sphere.
" If this be all of it," said he,
" How wide is yonder rolling sea ?"
The man of olden time, we said,
Did wear no crown upon his head,
His sway was of a nobler kind
Than mere brute force ; he was design'd
A prince indeed, in realms of mind,
And gifted with a faith that dared
To hope where others had despaired.
In early youth he lov'd to roam
Far from his poor, yet sunny home ;
Upon the heaving ocean's tide
Was his delight and joy to ride,
Nor carelessly and unconcern'd
But ev'ry page of Nature turn'd,
As in her volume he discern'd
That mighty truth whose ray of light
Turn'd night to day, made darkness bright;
That shook all preconceiv'd belief
And vaunting *savans* brought to grief.
Convinced that it was true, he brought
His theory before the Court ;
And ne'er before did kingly ear
A tale so strange receive and hear.

II.

What realms of beauty are unfurl'd
In that one word—another World ;
What visions crowd before the eye,

Of fields and flowers, fruits and sky;
Of rivers laving, fertile plains;
Of waving fields of golden grain;
Of beings of celestial mould
Whose beauty mortal never told!
What balmy sweets perfume the air!
What strains of music floating there!
Such dreams as this and thoughts sublime
Did urge the man of olden time
To dare the perils of the wave,
Where spooks and horrid monsters lave:
Their "slimy sides" and "bar the way,"
As ancient tars were wont to say.
The haughty monarch, with a sneer,
Bade him begone; he could not hear
A tale so wild, nay even thought
Derangement all the scheme had wrought.
"No more," quoth he, "demented man,
All common sense rejects thy plan.
A poet's most ecstatic flight
Did never soar to such a height,
Nor his imagination swept,
So wildly even while he slept.
Another World! There is but one
Beyond the sphere we dwell upon.
I have no vessel which can bear,
Nor aught to waft thy spirit there.
My ships have plough'd the briny main
In search of land; the search was vain.
The sea is but a liquid hell,
Where *spooks* and horrid monsters dwell;
Dismiss thy visionary scheme,
As shadows of an idle dream."

'Tis thus the vulgar mind is prone
To judge all others by its own,

Nor deem that deeper minds may scan
Beyond their own contracted span;
Whose own, enamour'd of its ease,
But clings to what it feels and sees:
Contented with the dusty way,
That millions plodded ere its day;
Unknowing genius can create,
And people realms and worlds innate;
Nor that its eagle eye discerns
Those very realms for which it yearns;
Nor that its wing can cleave their way,
Thro' mists of folly in its day;
Nor that its soul was sent from Him
Who made the glowing Cherubim;
That it, per force, must upward rise,
Unhappy save in native skies.
No wonder then such minds explore,
And create worlds not seen before,
Since dunces rule and fools obey
In that wherein their bodies stay.

III.

Oh! Woman, made alone to bless
Humanity in sore distress,
Thy glory runs commensurate
With man in destiny or fate;
Thro' thee the man of mind prevailed
While vaunting *savans* him assailed.
Let future cynics who would vex
Their souls about " the weaker sex,"
Think of all worlds so far as known,
She figures first, as facts have shown,
And hath by virtue of her plea
Of innate curiosity,
Aton'd for more than half the bell,
Accruing since her Mother fell.

At last our hero steers amain
The trackless paths of ocean's plain,
So far as human eye could pierce,
Appear'd a liquid universe,
Yet firm he stood, nor him subdue
The menace of the craven crew,
Who begg'd him with beseeching cries,
His course to steer for native skies.
The leeks and onions sweeter far
To them appear'd than glory's star;
A life of ease, a death obscure,
A body rich, a spirit poor;
Grant such but these, they ask no more.
But more will nobler natures crave
Than earth can give, or ever gave;
The beautiful, the true, the just,
Such things as seldom dwell in dust.
Born to command, he kept them down,
As best he might by smile or frown,
Or sought at times to stimulate
Their sense of pride, one thing innate,
At least in human kind, without
One single cause to bring about.
The malefactor, thief and liar,
The vilest wench whom rakes admire,
Can all else bear, all else condone,
Their pride you must not trample on
Relentless Tyrant, without tears
For any of thy worshippers;
In vain the agonizing waist
To half its usual size comprest;
Poor toes that wanting room ride double,
He only laughs at all your trouble,
And thus doth silly pride pervert
Our very virtues; we exert
Our starving souls to feed on wind
And leave the nobler things behind.

IV.

Here, Reader, let thy fancy stop
With Moses on the mountain top,
And view with him the goodly sight
Of Canaan from the mountain height.
Yet deem not Moses stood aghast
At what before his vision pass'd,
For he, the first of mortal race,
Had talk'd with God, as face to face,
While all around the mountain shone
Celestial light from Heav'ns throne,
And little beauty earth e'er brings
To him who sees celestial things.
Then turn to him who now surveys
The mighty dream of other days,
But real now, thyself imbue
With what he felt at such a view.
Ah! tell me not of battles won;
Of deeds that were by valor done;
Of braying bugles that proclaim
Achievement of a mighty fame!
Alone in some neglected spot
A sister weeps for brothers not:
Torn in instant from her side,
The husband from the tender bride;
A Mother's wail ascends the sky—
"My Son, my Son: alas, to die!
Sole object of declining years,
No triumphs stay my burning tears;
While booming guns commemorate
The victory, I mourn thy fate."
Not thus with him who steer'd amain
The pathless waste. No sense of pain
Disturbs his soul as he surveys
The sight whose smallest glimpse outweighs
The days of darkness, hours of pain,

When supplication seem'd in vain,
When sceptred dullness block'd the way
That made the darkness into day;
No more the agony severe
Of hope deferr'd from year to year,
But feeling such as angels might
E'en envy tho' in Heaven's sight:
'Tis past, at length they saw the shore
No Eastern eye had seen before;
From ship to ship the accents fly—
"Land, Ho! Land, Ho!!" as ev'ry eye
Was strain'd as tho' it would defy
The sense of sight, nor yet believe,
So loth is Dullness to receive
The truth; but soon the very shore
Heaves into sight—they doubt no more.
Their curses into praises turn,
Of one whom late they wish'd to spurn,
And men, all mutinous before,
Then knelt his pardon to implore.
Oh! wretched World, indeed thou art
A syren in thy very heart.
The child of genius, when unknown,
In asking bread receives a stone;
Yet turn at once in fame complete
And pour thy treasures at his feet;
A smile, a token, or a nod,
Ye reverence as ye would a god
From one perhaps who oft before
Was rudely driven from your door,
Or made the butt of ridicule,
By stupid ass and silly fool,
Whose sole invention to annoy
Those whom their wit cannot destroy.

The calm is sweet when storms are gone,
The darkness ushers in the dawn,

As thro' the gates of death and pain,
The soul remounts to life again.
So now the long expected hour,
That ushers in the day of power,
When genius shall confirm its sway,
With beams of intellectual day ;
Not like some baleful comet hurl'd
Thro' space to awe a guilty world ;
No meteor in whose flashes shine
Malignant light, or fell design ;
But like the clear, resplendent sun,
That gladdens all it shines upon ;
That thaws the rills and frozen lakes
And in Dame Nature's womb awakes
The germs of life until they burst
The bonds, and at her bosom nurs'd,
Expand, adorn and beautify
The field, the forest, and the sky.

V.

The night was dark, the sky was black
With tempest, waves were giving back
The whispers of the viewless wind.
The watchful petrel sought to find
A refuge where her fragile form
Might shun the fury of the storm.
Who e'er hath at midnight stood
By window looking to the wood,
And watch'd of all sublimest sight
A tempest gath'ring in the night ?
Hath seen when lurid lightings broke,
The figure of the gnarled oak,
Of verdue stript, devoid of bark,
Its naked limbs white, stiff, and stark,
Stretch'd out as if to supplicate
The God of storms to spare it yet.

The lofty poplar's stately head
Moves nervously as if the dread
Of sudden ruin lurk'd apace
To hurl it from its rooted place.
With sudden scream the startled bird
Flies wildly from its nest; the herd
Of lowing kine with tail distent
Around the compass'd fold lament.
The snorting steed the scene excites
To use his heels in circling flights,
Till suddenly, when all is still
Except the growling of the rill,
Disputing with a stubborn stone
That blocks its pathway to the throne
Of ocean's empire—till a flash
Of blazing lightning with the crash
Of loudest thunder seems to shake
The pillars of this globe opaque.
Then comes the fiercely driven rain,
Like pebbles rattling on the pane;
While flapping blinds, as swift they veer
On rusty hinges, fright the ear
With sudden knocks as if they were
Flung madly with the storm-king's might
At him who dares look on the sight.
A moment more the windy hell
Is at its height.　Sulphurous smell
Impregns the air as if the cave
Of hell itself the odor gave.
A flash!—behold the gnarled oak
Is riven by the lightning's stroke;
While concomitant thunder shakes
The solid earth itself, and makes
Cups click as if a drunkard's ghost
Were striking them proposing toast.

*　　　*　　　*　　　*　　　*　　　*　　　*

An hour past, and all is still
Except the roaring of the rill,
Evincing anger or surprise,
Or joy at its sudden size;
And rolls exultingly along,
And vents its joy in its song.
The massive clouds are pil'd away,
But still the zigzag lightnings play
In sportive shapes upon their breast
Till finally they sink to rest.
Then star by star peeps out to look
Abash'd on scenes their light forsook.
Pale Luna brightly shines apace
As if the rain had washed her face;
The air is redolent with sweets
Of battered roses, whose retreats
The ruthless storm-king swept among,
And from their fragile tendrils wrung,
The lily pale from off its stem,
And rose to deck his diadem.
Torn nature smoothes her wrinkled brow
And silence reigns supremely now.
This seen, at once forsake the shore
In fancy for the ocean's roar;
Be present, in the tempest share;
Behold the darken'd skies prepare
For battle, see the black array
Of angry clouds, the vaulting spray,
That like a giant, leaps on high,
To bid defiance to the sky.
The sails are flapping like the wings
Of Angels, or mysterious things,
As if they were enjoin'd to swell
The chorus of the liquid hell.
The groaning bars and shrinking beams
Grate harshly on the ear, and teems

The deep with monsters' horrid forms,
That are not seen except in storms.
The creaking cordage adds its might
To swell the chorus of affright;
Imagine next the human freight
Of agony, bewailing fate,
Imploring ev'ry patron saint,
Or rushing wildly making feint
Of self-destruction yet refrain
And cowards turn and hope again.

* * * * * * *

The calm is sweet when storms are gone,
The darkest hour proceeds the dawn—
And when he mounts with dripping wings,
Most glorious of created things,
The king of day, the storm is spent,
And clouds are swept in banishment.

VI.

Ashore! the night's disaster past,
The promis'd haven reach'd at last!
All that was madness just before
Is genius now, and none forebore
That tribute to superior mind,
That men acknowledge when they find
They must, if not become by rule,
Themselves the butts of ridicule.
A rugg'd path is his to tread,
Who is by inspiration led;
The thorns of envy and deceit
Must pierce his unprotected feet,
His aching heart no solace know
From those above, nor those below;
Above the hiss of ridicule,
Beneath the hootings of the fool,
And as he probes the rotten core

Of systems false, at least a score
Of Blanches, Trays, and Sweethearts yelp
Most piteously to spare their whelp;
The storms of calumny and wrath
Frown blackly o'er his lonely path;
Malicious wit exerts its best
To pluck a feather from his crest;
While ostentatious dullness bars
His upward bent and thanks its stars
That it was born without the curse
Of insanity—or worse.
Quacks, charlatans and parvenens
All band together, lest they lose,
As did their type, Demetrius,
The sacred art of cheating us,
Whilst others, as he strips the skin
That asses hide their ears within,
Look on it as a deadly sin.
Thus throughout life creative mind
Must battle fiercely with its kind,
To die at length (too oft the case)
In cold neglect, or worse, disgrace,
While critics fatten on the spoils
He leaves behind of all his toils,
Extol the genius that could dare
To tread where weaker men forbear,
And in his ev'ry feature find,
(By some cheap picture left behind)
The traces of a giant mind.
These, and no doubt a thousand more
The hero of "Eureka" bore,
Yet lovely woman, be it said,
That he was from thy bounty fed,
And Isabella shares the fame
That clusters 'round Columbus' name.

E

VII.

THE MORAL OF EUREKA.

Since great Galileo began
The idea of the wondrous plan,
How worlds revolv'd and planets steer'd
By settled laws that have not veei'd,
From orbits fix'd a breadth of hair,
Your would-be wits have not been rare,
And shallow critics rais'd a shout
At things they nothing knew about,
Incapable of comprehension
And destitute of all invention,
Have made themselves but silly asses,
To him whose mind their own surpasses.
So far the contrast would provoke,
Such laughter as the gods would choke,
And genius must at all events
Crack first the skull of common sense,
To make more room, ere it begin,
To let a genuine idea in,
So must it also overturn
Another's hobby ere it earn
Its meed of praise, as if the field
Of science were not made to yield
Its hidden store for all that seek,
Be they Scythian or Greek;
Yet genius neither recks nor feels
The little curs which snap its heels.
Earth ever had two doubtful chaps
Call'd "Peradventure" and "Perhaps."
Tho' bad enough, yet they are better
Than stupid dullness, their begetter;
These, ever since they first existed,
Had knotty brains which doubt had twisted,
And so since man was first created,

This twain, tho' superannuated,
Have hard heads still, tho' they should be
As "soft as mud ;" for blows you see
Have fall'n on them thick and fast,
And "Progress" knocks them down at last.
These be the little wits that give
Their firm opinion that we live
In a degenerate day, and mourn
The "good old days" when hay and corn
Brought better prices, nay they deem
The Devil first invented steam,
The roaring engines that propel
The cosy car, first us'd in hell,
That one in league with Lucifer,
A patent got to use it here.
Think of it ye plodding fools,
Who hamper genius with your rules,
How on a time in conclave met
A would-be knowing pious set,
With solemn mien and scowling glance
For one who ventur'd to advance
An idea, which approving time
Them dunces prov'd, and him sublime.
Look at your brethren as they sit
Thro' centuries, the butts of wit,
And, worse by far the ridicule,
That arms each atheistic fool,
Who by a sally or a point
Knocks all your Scripture out of joint,
And cut your doctrines half in two
By witticism or BON-MOT.

   *   *   *   *   *   *   *

It is the proof of master mind,
To see where others are but blind ;
To travel tracks before unknown,
To create systems of its own,

To doubt all things till proof be shown;
To shatter creeds or systems built
On superstition, error, guilt,
With conscious rectitude of aim,
To bear the brunt, despise the shame,
That open warfare ever makes
When it the props of error shakes.

RICHARD VULGUS, ESQ.

A TALE OF MODERN SOCIETY.

Sir Richard lived up town—that is to say,
A denizen was of "Fifth Avenue,"
To social heavens this is the proper way,
The way quite oft to Purgatory too.
As Richard's youth with poverty was cursed,
Perhaps he had his purgatory first.

Sir Richard was descended from a class
Call'd poor, but honest; their history
Cannot be known, therefore we let it pass
Just as we would another mystery;
Suffice to say, his lineage began
Somewhere in the history of man.

Sir Richard's Father made no pretension
To gentle blood, lived and died contented
At boiling soap; this is no mean invention,
For vulgar blood, which cannot be prevented,
Does not affect the skin; but good old soap
Will cleanse a rascal and benefit a Pope.

Père Richard gather'd, by "dint of hook and crook,"
A tolerable fortune from soap and suds,
Yet never dream'd his hopeful Son would look
For rank and station along with other "bloods."
He was mistaken : parents mostly are,
In leaving offspring with too great a share.

His Father left, as we have said above,
His riches to his Son, enough to start
An enterprising man, (we always love
To specify) this is the mystic art
That makes a poet; but it suits us here,
To use it in making our story clear.

Sir Richard's youth was spent among the rabble,
With no refinement save what comes of soap,
His good old *Père* no *penchant* had to dabble
In classic streams, had read no lines in Pope,
Nor known of Milton—crazy George the Third,
The only King of which he ever heard.

But Richard was an economic man,
His wealth expanded in proportion too ;
By perseverance in the proper plan,
He soon became as rich as any Jew,
And this of course was follow'd by effects
Which prudish poverty ne'er once suspects.

Our hero's wife was of the common run
Of ordinary women ; very fond
Of telling husbands all things should be done
In full accordance with, though not beyond,
Their proper limits—this is what she meant :
Soap boiling was no office for a gent.

We forgot to notice an essential
Fact, which may be relevant just here,
One often pays for being deferential;
Silence has cost some novel-makers dear,
When they are forc'd to thrust upon the stage
Some one not mention'd in a former page.

The fact in question, Richard had been blest
With pledges maternal—a Daughter, Son.
We mention this because we deem it best
To aid the story we have just begun.
These little things all help us to evolve
The social problem we are now to solve.

Sir Richard was unletter'd, never had
A literary turn; above we said,
His was indeed a most illiterate "dad,"
Soap fill'd his purse and occupied his head.
His Son, of course, regarded with suspicion,
All learning foreign to his dad's condition.

This being so, by no means does it follow
He was a fool because he had no taste
For literature; some heads are hollow,
Or empty rather, though they have been graced
With varied learning. Of all the fools,
He is the worst who issues from the schools.

What native spark he may have had at first
Is smother'd and extinguish'd, sterile land,
By being cultur'd but becomes more curst,
And erudition one cannot command
Is worse than none, an over-loaded cart,
That stands stone still, or breaks down at the start.

Pardon this digression, if it can be
A sin to pardon when we step aside
To pluck an apple, (an idea from the tree
That is "*outre mer*,") still it may decide,
Cut short, or snap the thread of narrative,
And not be worth the trouble that we give.

But "*au revoir!*" Sir Richard, we have said,
Was a man unletter'd; that is no matter,
For one may have high notions in his head
To dip his spoon into the social platter,
"Top of the pot," the precious "upper ten,"
Who order fashion, while they ruin men. .

The women, (and kind Heav'n help them all,)
This weakness have much greater than the men :
"*Elite soirees*" and a selected ball,
Their summits of ambition : the sword and pen,
Belong of course, (and who would wish to hinder,)
To bipeds only of another gender.

Now, Madame Vulgus, pining day by day ,
To leave the suds for good society,
Essay'd her lord, a woman has a way
Of doing all things with propriety,
Her reasons are ingenious; they can steer
'Twixt Charybdis and Sylla without fear.

The weakest point their eyes are sure to see,
Then pour on this their concentrated force,
Till stupid husbands cannot find a plea,
And then—"Yes, Dear, it shall be done of course."
Her warfare is unceasing. Who could find
A safe retreat if woman had a mind !

Sir Richard sold his vats, his own good will
And bought a house, as we have said before,
In fashionable quarters; a bitter pill
To high-minded *nabobs* who lived next door.
What should they do; turn up their haughty noses.
And, like a Jew, swear—"in the name of Moses."

A Music Teacher—salary immense,
None need apply who cannot also bring
The best of reference, as the expense
Is not an item,—taught to play and sing
A girl and boy,—call at ten o'clock
At Number ——, in front of Astor's block.

This the *denoument*, a needy creature
To train young hopefuls; the curtain rises,
The scenery was charming, ev'ry feature
Partaking of refinement, sweet surprises
Of expectant lovers, all that art could do
For naked walls came boldly out to view.

The little Cupids, all in sportive shapes
Adorn'd the mantels, marble-tops were laden
With precious stones, all purchas'd on the capes
Whence diamonds come from—the earthly Aiden,
The floor with Turky—while Venetian blinds,
These beauties hid from vulgar, prying minds.

The library, too, was royal in its line;
Shakspeare in calf conspicuously shone;
While Pope and Milton, scarcely less divine,
Along with Dryden—hundreds more unknown
To their possessor, grac'd his costly shelves,
Looking like apologies for themselves.

Creative spirits, only born to shine,
Consign'd to darkness once unknown to Thee!
Oh, Genius mighty! did thy soul divine
In what strange company its thoughts should be!
Pope's Dunciad, "Perditus Paradisus"
And classic Virgil, "*quae numine laesos*."

But so it was, Sir Richard was inflated,
His "better half" was more than half distracted.
Of course they thought such things were calculated
To purchase caste: this farce cannot be acted
Till time shall teach the fashionable arts,
And make the actors familiar with their parts.

Madame Vulgus was unhappy, who could be
In her case happy; fish, themselves, on land
Were just as likely. Their place a fool can see
Is water only; on the other hand,
When Madame Vulgus left her suds and soap,
She lost true happiness to live on hope.

It takes at least a century or two
For vulgar folk, howe'er rich they be
To purge themselves, and act as others do,
Whose birth and rank have serv'd to keep them free
From clownishness. All this may seem unjust,
But so says Nature, and obey we must.

She had to steer 'twixt Sylla and Charybdis;
Incontinently curs'd by those forsaken;
Some vaguely hinted either that or this,
Explain'd the reason she her course had taken,
While those she sought said with strict propriety
That soap was good, but it was not society.

"The upper ten," a circle overnice,
Display'd no sign, no wish, to fraternize,
But Walpole says that each man has his price;
And on this point Sir Walpole never lies:
Who does it first, ah hereat was the rub
That kept the rats from jumping in the tub.

Society, like sheep, will hesitate
To leap a fence—that is the social line,
Until the leader, without regard to fate,
Jumps headlong over; they pronounce it "line"
And follow forthwith, each seeming to outvie
The other's haste; this no one can deny.

Death is a leveller, so is money,
Effete aristocrats must all confess,
That credit has but little ceremony
For well-bred persons when moneyless.
The butcher's bill; a hundred others too,
Are punctually call'd for, no matter who.

Admission then among the chosen few
Was made a matter of pure speculation,
The women oppos'd it—they always do,
Then yield and mourn a blighted reputation,
Yet always have some artifice at hand
To reconcile the ground on which they stand.

The bonds are broken, an invite to a *Soiree;*
"Pray what is that?" suggested Madame V.
Sir Richard does not know; the teacher may,
So he is call'd to tell what it may be.
This being done, the notes of preparation
Made Richard's house a scene of animation.

They must appear of course in *a la mode*;
But Madame Vulgus had not studied French,
Yet she succeeded; no woman ever showed
A lack of talent here: a silly wench
Soon knows for certain what man can only guess,
The puzzling mysteries of the female dress.

But Madame Vulgus had her milliner,
Richard, of course, his skillful tailor too.
With each of these they mutually confer
About the work they gave them now to do.
This being done, when lo, another point
Contriv'd to knock them both quite out of joint.

Sir Richard could not read, therefore could not write,
His better half was like him ; here was trouble,
An answer must be given this invite,
Or else a pin would prick the social bubble;
Their new born hopes would all at once collapse
Alone from one, of poverty's mishaps.

"Call for the teacher," shouted Richard, " he
Can settle this, we'll give him extra pay
To keep his mouth shut." " What says Madame V.
Are we to do when he is gone away."
"The best we can, My Dear; the times demand,
We use him now, while he is at our hand."

The teacher came, though seeming somewhat sour,
These interruptions were not hard to bear,
Did they not happen a dozen times an hour ;
The children too, entrusted to his care,
Grew quite unruly—a thing to be expected
When left alone, or worse than that, neglected.

A hint is oft the parent of suggestion,
Suggestion oft a real idea brings,
And trifles too, (of which there is no question)
Reveal the way to dark and hidden things;
Sir Isaac Newton, gravity and all,
First found the clue in seeing apples fall.

We like digressions, though at times they be,
Both witless and prosy, and yet we know
The sweetest fruit grows on forbidden tree,
At least mankind have e'er deem'd it so,
And sought out paths beyond the beaten way
That sweating millions plodded ere their day.

But to the idea, lest we should forget,
Some private person must at once be had
To answer *billet doux,* his son as yet
Had not lore sufficient to serve his dad,
Besides a Secretary, no doubt augments
The social status of all would-be gents.

Madame Vulgus donn'd her fashionable dress,
Which barely hid—Oh, well we need not say.
Her husband gave some tokens of distress,
And, one may add, a little of dismay.
He had not learn'd that modesty and sense
Are now-a-days in the pluperfect tense.

"Pray is it modest, Dear, to dress that way;
It scarcely hides your person, can't you see?"
"Don't be so stupid, this is what they say,"
Suggested Madame, "the *elight: that's me,*
Would sooner die (now this may seem a joke,)
If fashion said not, than to wear a cloak."

Now man can be a most provoking ass
In woman's estimation if he choose,
By interdicting social whims that pass
For current coin. Why should one refuse,
Who went so far in fashionable folly
And thereby make his lady melancholy ?

And Madame Vulgus took no middle ground,
At least in eating fashionable crow ;
Her husband was of course in duty bound,
Whether he had an appetite or no.
But tastes are soon acquir'd, we may hate
The very milk that fed our infant state.

But Madame's turn was next, the swallow-tail
In due time came, a fashionable cut ;
Then Madame's tongue, (no woman's tongue can fail
At such a crisis,) found pretext to put
Some telling thrusts : " My Dear, now don't you see,
If you wear that you should not rail at me !"
        *   *   *   *   *   *   *

And now on high, the pompous driver sat,
With whip in hand and ready for behest ;
A feather grac'd his shining beaver hat,
While polish'd brass adorn'd his purple vest.
Emblem mute of patience and of pride
Or rather *hauteur* and something else beside.

Crack went the whip—off went the prancing steeds,
The shining wheels sang as they whirl'd along,
O'er cobble stones and up a street that leads
Right into Heaven—no, that is rather strong—
But right into the long desir'd spot,
Where everything but money is forgot.
        F

The trip is up—a stately mansion rears
A front imposing, which can well compare
With that of Richard's; so the Madame fears
The inside may be better. " Why did Richard spare
A single thing that he was told to buy ?
He did not know ; " that was the reason why.

Thus contrast digs, alas, a deeper hell !
It caus'd from Heav'n the arch-fiend to fall;
One should content himself in doing well,
And, having much, not hanker after all.
But this remark has been in vogue before;
We leave it with—Sir Richard at the door.

Now up the steps with trembling frames they go;
Ring at the door—look in each other's eyes
As if some thought were lurking there ; but no,
Both stood like stones, and neither could surmise
The other's idea: Richard thought of soap,
The Madame lost in reveries of hope.

Obsequious usher, soon in state prepar'd,
White apron tied around his slender waist,
Came to the door, and "Please give me your card
To take forthwith, kind Sir, to Madame Taste;
Your card, you see, once being taken in,
Where I leave off the Madame will begin."

Sir Richard was dumbfounded, gave a look
At Madame Vulgus, more than seem'd to say
"What shall we do; have you no hook nor crook
For this dilemma, you not find a way ?"
The Madame's cheek was slightly ting'd with amber
From this detention in an antechamber.

She call'd the driver; he at once obeyed,
"Go quick," says she, "here is an extra quarter,
And get my cards; inquire for the maid
To give them to you, or else my pretty daughter."
This done, she gave a sigh of sweet relief,
The waiter star'd--this was "another leaf."

The driver came with the desir'd note,
Sir Richard took, but did not take a glance,
And if he had, why since he never wrote
And could not read—but an unlucky chance—
The hasty driver had only brought a card
Which read "R. Vulgus, Dealer in Bones and Lard."

The waiter took it, this was his duty,
To Madame Taste. "A joy forever,"
Says the poet Keats, "is a thing of beauty."
"This billet-doux, I hope that it may never!"
Says Madame T. without a thought just then
Concerning Keats, "confound such vulgar men."

"Why wife," suggested that unlucky limb
Of trees parental, call'd in ridicule
"A doating husband;" "You remember him
For whom in special you must drop your rule,
That honest burgher, who by proper care
In boiling bones, has been invited here!"

"Oh, yes; what shall I say? This detention,
I fear, has wounded them," so out she flew.
"Why, Mrs. V., why did you not mention
Your name to the servant? Sir Richard, you
Should not have been so backward; don't you see
How such a thing might cause hard thoughts of me!"

In Richard went, the Madame on his arm,
A nervous thrill shot through his stalwart frame,
The Madame's bosom beat with soft alarm,
Her cheek at least had lost its amber flame,
Brought face to face with those imperial gods,
Who hold the science of *conges*, bows and nods.

First, on the right, ubiquitous Grundy sat,
And next to her the gushing Jenkins gaped,
Then Miss La Mode, or something else like that,
All wrapp'd in silks and dress'd in such a shape
That one would think she carried on her back
Enough to fill a first-class peddler's pack.

And Charles Augustus, he of fragile form,
With sweet blue eyes and whiskers wax'd with care,
Who took in youth some maiden's heart by storm
By his graces only, a thing most rare,
Unaided by money, Charles won his way,
And married her who was an heiress *nee*.

These, in their turn, were each one introduced
To Richard and his lady, a host of others,
Mosquitos fashionable, who deduc'd
A scanty living from their wealthy brothers,
And sang a ditty like them, to earn a supper,
Flirt with the girls, and quote some lines from Tupper.

Poor Richard was silent, he dare not launch
Into the sea of fashionable folly
Lest he should flounder, Madame's cheek should blanch
With fear, as she seem'd quite melancholy;
The social whales might swim out in the deep,
But he and she both near the shore would keep.

But Richard was no fool; his common sense
Avail'd him more than all the books supply,
Altho' he knew no past, no future tense
So far as Murray, yet his mind could vie
In native force with those who can but quote
Some choice bits that Pope or Dryden wrote.

This was his mistake, a common error
To deem ourselves unhappy in a state
Where fortune plac'd us, or live in terror
Of foolish laws and seek to regulate
Our lives and conduct by rules invented
For fops and asses, and like demented,

But virtue, true nobility of mind,
Is not confin'd to excepted classes,
Nor wit, nor talent do we mostly find
Amongst the most aristocratic asses;
With few exceptions, all their minds can get
Within them is, a point of etiquette.

Simplicity and greatness are twin-born ;
Gravity in the features of a donkey
Is most apparent ; a mimic scorn
Belongs to fops as well as to a monkey.
Cease talking then about the "social status"
Till Darwin's apes have ceas'd their grinning at us.

And we have seen a youth with purpose high
And noble soul repuls'd with sullen scorn,
When fops and fools alone were sitting by,
And made the slight still harder to be borne,
Yet this is just according to a code
Made by a few, the brainless *a la mode*.

Ye precious few, with good opinions laden
Of your own importance, your highest aim
Is to seduce some artless simple maiden,
And then desert her, leave her in her shame
With no resource but death, or what is worse,
To her parents lost—to herself—a curse!

And where is he, destroyer of her peace,
Foul murd'rer; we will write it to their shame,
'Tis a mark of honor, smiles did not cease,
Foul as you are, yet still *creme de la creme*
Could not afford to lose a shining light,
Nor part with one whose vices were so slight.

Abject is he whom that imperious fraud
Rules like a slave, that soul can feel
No high delight, true character outlawed;
With him 'tis worse to labor than to steal.
Yet these are they who mould the social state
With unpaid ushers scowling at the gate.

This is the class whose infinite precision
In points pertaining to the social scale,
Have won at least a genuine derision
From all but fools; but fools prevail
In point of numbers: till all such are dead
It will continue—no more need be said.

We now return to Richard and his lady.
See how they act in such a heavy play,
Light as it seems to one who has already
Been duly school'd to act the proper way!
'Tis heavy work for one whose youth is spent
Beyond the pale that constitutes a gent.

Sir Richard Vulgas had not learn'd as yet
His antecedents were as good as'theirs;
Frogs, *pere* tadpole, would willingly forget,
But others don't, and supercilious airs
But counterfeit the real manly mein
Which upstarts never feel, but may have seen.

True blood at least is like unto Burgundy,
The bottles never the taste alone can tell
The genuine from counterfeit, but Madame Grundy
Would make believe some fashionable swell
Of " gentle blood "—Oh, Heaven, save the phrase—
Applied to snobs in these degenerate days.

A curse on Darwin, him whose creed unsettles
Aristocratic faith; for if his scheme be true
Mankind were monkeys: here's a theme that nettles
Our high-born pride; this thing will never do,
Unless he prove and demonstrate in shape
Elite there were among our genus ape.

'Tis needless to say in all crowds we meet,
Had we the wish such secrets to unearth,
Some things were found not positively sweet
For those too prone to advertise their worth.
What odds is it, provided one is just,
'Twixt hoeing corn or holding worlds in trust?

A silent tongue oft makes a wiser head
So we are told; we will not vouch for this:
One may be mute and silly too, we read
Some choice proofs how one can judge amiss.
Still Richard and Madame had enough to say,
Not at that time, but at a future day.

The die was cast; he could not now retrace
His former life, that lay beyond the flood,
He dare not mention a word about his race;
We mean of course his parentage or blood,
Tho' chimney-sweeps could call at least a dozen,
If brought to life by the sweet name of cousin.

But Madame was in ecstasies, had found
A recognition which she did not hope;
No words were said that could inflict a wound,
'Mid so much talk no one had utter'd soap;
Music, mirth, and soul-inspiring wine,
Had swept away the all dividing line.

Duets, quartettes in turn, she all refused,
She had a cold, they must excuse her now.
Tho' not familiar with all terms they used,
She knew enough, could make a graceful bow,
And tell with ease a fashionable lie:
This is an art that all can learn who try.

Poor Richard sat and utter'd not a word;
He felt dismay'd: what husband would not feel
Some faint misgivings if he only heard
The half of this, unless his heart were steel?
Here was the one whom he could once adore,
Acting the fool and lying by the score.

He was a sadder, not a wiser man,
Had he been so he would have stayed at home,
Nor let his wife adopt another plan,
Or choose a sphere whence shame can only come,
Made her to know true happiness depends
On tried acquaintance, not with foreign friends.

Her life henceforth was one incessant round
Of fashionable folly; ended her career
In dissipation, but Richard found
The sweetest joy vouchsafed a mortal here
Is with the friends who cherish us in youth,
Rough though they be their love indeed is truth.

THE STORY OF PERDITUS.

A TALE OF REAL LIFE.

"I am an outcast. All decent society
　　Has spew'd me out as a thing unclean;
I am not famous for strict sobriety
　　And other virtues equally as mean.
This will appear as I propose to give
My own history in this narrative.

"Well, I was born—it does not matter where—
　　I merely say it to begin my story;
My birth was humble, yet my lineage fair,
　　Till I disgraced it of its pride and glory.
Mine is no antiquated tale; I fell
From no line illustrious—no curs can yell.

"My youth was spent, as I was very poor,
　　In hoeing corn and other vulgar turns
As served to keep a famine from my door,
　　And set to rights a parent's small concerns;
Such as his stock, the number very slight,
I tended to, and chopped the wood at night.

"About sixteen I found my way to school,
   The world at last was opening to my view,
And no one shuts his eyes, except a fool,
   And misses chances as he passes through.
Good intentions are pleasurable things
To be discussed by rogues and thieving rings.

"Old Squire Legens was a learned man,
   Read Plutarch's Lives and Machiavelli's Prince,
The ancient feuds of ev'ry Highland clan,
   And ev'ry novel bound and written since
Adam first figur'd as hero in the first,
And married Eve—as usual, got the worst.

"The school-house a shanty—perhaps a hut,
   But take your choice, call it as you please—
A wooden chimney, always full of soot,
   The underpinning mostly hogs and fleas,
The scholars all a teacher could desire,
Whose chief ambition to make a dunce or liar.

" With dignity the learned Legens sat
   Upon his throne, a crazy wooden chair,
Bottom'd with splits, and issued his fiat,
   Which made on end each individual hair
To stand erect. I've read this line somewhere,
In " Whitman's Leaves," if not it should be there.

"Cowhide and birch contain the first resort
   That fogies use in managing a school,
They much prefer to sending a report
   To use the rod; no boy is a mule
Unless a brute shall choose to make him one
By beating him; this is the way it's done.

"Talk of mosquitoes, bed-bugs, flies and fleas,
    Of being bor'd by some stupid dunce,
And first be thrash'd, then lectured, on your knees,
    You'll not exchange the punishment but once.
No wonder, then, from all such schools as this
That rascals come and turn their steps amiss.

"A lie would save where truth would only fail;
    What boy, then, with little moral sense,
Would hesitate to tell a lying tale
    To save his hide, altho' at truth's expense?
Yet this is done and mankind wonder why
That Nature gives propensities to lie.

"Book learning, however, is not essential
    To common sense, nor common sense to it,
For one may be, (we say this deferential,)
    An ass, altho' his head be full of wit,
But not his own, but borrow'd from a stall,
Where luckless wits with all their wisdom crawl.

"The Squire was a genius of this kind,
    Original only in the application
Of another's idea; not sufficient mind
    For that rare talent call'd adaptation;
A dunce, a *doctrinaire*, a mere buffoon,
Who tried the stars, tho' stricken by the moon.

"Now this old cob was pious in his way,
    And 'pious in his way' includes a deal
Of devious twisting from what they say,
    That Christians are suppos'd to act and feel,
Still woman and cards were never in his line;
For book-worms rarely in these graces shine.

"His vices mostly were negative in kind,
    That is to say, he lack'd the moral force
To sin outright, yet devilish shrewd to find
    Some text in writ to justify his course,
Which was comprised, we say it in a lump,
'By whipping the Devil around the stump.'

"Here was I taught the elements of vice,
    The letters in the alphabet of sin,
And progress'd finely, stopping once or twice,
    To see how best my career to begin.
I was no meaner taken from the start,
Than other lads—I owe it all to art.

"But why excuses to those I most despise?
    They ruined me ere I had injur'd them,
They taught me first to value cheats and lies;
    They made the crown I wear the diadem;
They taught me, too, (and could I hope for less,)
Crimes are forgiven when one achieves success.

"Hypocrisy only is said to be
    A tribute forced, which Vice to Virtue pays.
I am no hypocrite, this a fool can see,
    The class I represent, no class that prays
In public loudly, straightway condescend
To steal a farthing or to rob a friend.

"Still I have no apologies to make,
    My course is wrong, but still I wish to throw
On proper persons blame they blush to take;
    Vile as I am, I have the right to show
Some reason why so fallen I became,
And some excuse make for the sake of shame.

"My first encounter to which I did succumb,
   A trial was few mortals could resist;
Tho' I confess I must have been benumbed
   Till conscience smote me—here is where I missed;
For had I listen'd, doubtless I had been
A shining light among the moral men.

   *   *   *   *   *   *   *

"This was my first *fiasco:* youth is shy
   When it is caught to tempt the fates again;
And love, which has its inlet through the eye,
   Can be pluck'd out and give us little pain.
True hearts alone would ever volunteer
To love but one—mine changes ev'ry year.

"This scandal, of course, created quite a stir
   Among the moral ones, and I was sent
Forth in the world, without a word of cheer;
   Fine way, no doubt, to make a scamp repent,
And teach him morals: note and you will see
How much, at least, it benefitted me.

"Micawber was the fellow who invented
   The phrase of 'turning up;' I felt the force
Of his remarks, and altho' I dissented
   From his clause on 'waiting,' still this, of course
Is part of the programme, I did not wait,
But went at once, and herein give my fate:—

"Expelled from home I wander'd to the city
   In search of something. 'Cuts be as they may,'
One can somehow become a thing of pity,
   And thus be forc'd to sell himself for pay.
Conservative rascality pays the best—
Make all you can, but how, let that be guessed.

   G

"'Honesty is the best policy,' says
　The type supreme of dime-saving schools;
Such words were good in honest Franklin's days,
　When mankind heeded a set of moral rules
To guide them right, but the present rage
For lucre drives such maxims from the stage.

"Now I was born in that delightful clime
　That nourished him, and as a thing of course
Spent all spare moments, intervals of time,
　In reading proverbs from that moral source,
Which, like the Nile's, is undiscovered, yet
Poor Richard's Almanack the best to get.

"Who knows what grand creations are must know
　They spring from nothing, and labor to attain
To eminence, chance may make mountains so—
　Not men, for theirs must come from soul or brain,
Success alone is token of true merit,
Not blood, nor wealth—these may a fool inherit.

"A race of hypocrites from whence I sprung—
　I am not mealy-mouthed in what I say—
It matters little what may be said or sung,
　One has a right by virtue of his plea
Of outlawry to rail at what he pleases
And curse the race that gave him such diseases.

"The very soil I was fated to inhabit
　Was curs'd with barrenness—the sea-gull only
Sings the lullaby of the lonely rabbit
　That burrows in cliffs all ivyless and lonely.
Of course, therefore, our cunning must supply
What climate, soil, and Nature all deny.

"But I am wand'ring. I left myself,
 If I mistake not, in the busy city
In search of something to earn a little pelf,
 And thus avoid a vain appeal to pity.
Revolving schemes, at length I hit on this,
To be a peddler, no peddler comes amiss.

"I fill'd my pack and gaily sallied forth
 On fortune bent. The fates were in my favor.
I gull'd the silly, liv'd on bread and broth;
 My tastes were simple, for then no extra flavor
Had been requir'd by riotous delights;
I work'd by day, and staid in doors o'nights.

"In course of time—not that which Pollok wrote—
 I chang'd my programme, bought a spanking team
That carried more than what I us'd to *tote*
 Upon my back, and now began to dream
Of opulence. Nay, I had dream'd before;
Saw millions nodding to my slender store.

"My sphere, of course, I felt was too confined;
 My partners, too, of me suspicious grew,
For on computing cash accounts, they find,
 The peddler was the richer of the two.
They bought me out (it prov'd to be no pity)
For thirty thousand, and I left the city.

"As pilgrims up some mountain's side ascend,
 And stop anon to gaze on scenes below,
Review their path now smoother to its end,
 And thank the gods they have not far to go;
So I, content with money in my purse,
A moment paus'd my past life to rehearse.

"I summ'd it up with all its 'hooks and crooks,'
    From the first fiasco with Legins daughter,
And made *pensees* not borrow'd from the books
    That I had moved so far in muddy water.
It makes no matter, for comfort can be found
In such reflections, if we but look around.

"More sin is always done in making cash
    Than spending it, tho' some men differ here,
Yet all prime moves in a financial crash
    Are made by scoundrels, (stick a pin just there.)
And yet the world can always lend a smile
To guilty ones in adding to their pile.

"My course was crooked; nay more, wrong I mean;
    A deviation from the moral line
Which some men follow we have never seen
    But read about, and whose graces shine
In cheap editions of the Sunday School
Literature, written by an ass or fool.

"But I had made—it does not matter how—
    A pile at least to satisfy my need;
Could buy a country-seat and study now,
    Improve my mind, also my moral creed;
Turn philanthropist, or some other fraud,
Pretend simplicity, but feel a lord.

"I had been poor, and therefore keenly knew
    The bitter pangs that wait on rags and dirt,
Of begging heartless souls for work to do;
    The ceaseless struggle mind and limb exert;
To purchase what?—the offal they refuse,
And take such things as they disdain to use.

"Had also seen the sanctimonious sneer
    That greeted such as ever went to prayer.
They had no need of dirty paupers here,
    And seem'd surpris'd that God could need them there.
These things, with others, have driven me to take
My course in life, and money is my stake.

"But I am rich, and do not care a straw
    For such reflections as any choose to fling
From a disclosure of some little flaw
    That others pick. The bee has lost its sting.
I stand confest almost a millionaire;
This being so, a penny do I care.

"My steps to Gotham, the bulls and bears,
    Stock speculators, rail monopolies,
To rogues miscall'd (pardon me) millionaires,
    And other cheats that charm all human eyes.
A noble aim always deserves to be
Crown'd with success; it happen'd so to me.

"A millionaire, a leach in full repletion,
    With gain dishonest suck'd from rich and poor;
Whose monster piles ne'er dwindle to depletion,
    But river-like receiving more and more.
Their petty owners swell in proportion too.
Until an ass becomes a Richelieu.

"I was an adept, especially in stock,
    And came out best; sure always in the end
My cunning boat ne'er flounder'd on a rock,
    And never stranded on a dividend.
The secret was, I managed to preserve,
Where others quailed, a sure and steady nerve.

"I gain'd my point, became a millionaire,
　　Drank all the cups of sin and pleasure too ;
Yet did it all with such a merry air
　　That moral men were wont to praise me too.
Fair women own'd the power of my charms,
And welcom'd me (how else,) with open arms.

"Some surly souls heap'd curses on my head,
　　And flew to courts with malice and revenge.
The courts by me were duly rubb'd and fed ;
　　The judge could find no reason to impinge.
No judge e'er sees a culprit on the docket,
Who measures justice according to his pocket.

"High office never can elevate
　　A vulgar nature, and I knew these men
Were just as fond of greed and billingsgate,
　　Vile in the past, as much so now, as then ;
Exalted asses only seem immense
To idiots and others in want of sense.

"My moral creed, I must confess, is loose ;
　　My soul is of the coarsest grain I know ;
My neck, no doubt, would quite become a noose ;
　　My name suffice to bring out quite a show.
But I am safe—for this invent a phrase
Which you may read—'he never hangs who pays.'

"Tho' meanly vile I had not wholly lost
　　My self-respect ; perhaps the cringing crowd
Preserv'd it for me.　Much as I have tossed
　　In dissipation, some were always proud
To blow my trumpet.　Oh ! potent, heartless cash,
On poverty's bare back to lay the cruel lash !

"But hitherto I had escap'd detection ;
　Had gone in style, play'd billiards by the score,
Had lovely females to soothe me in dejection,
　Swells to court me, beggars to implore;
Had prayers invoking blessings on my head,
Women to love me knowing I was wed.

"Such treatment was too much, I do aver,
　For human nature at any length to stand.
I sometimes thought, I surely do not err,
　And became less coy, exhibiting my hand.
Success ever invariably blind
Alike the noble and ignoble mind.

"My drives were splendid; bays of speed and blood
　Seem'd proud to draw the car that me contained.
Why not ?　My bosom with a diamond stud
　Resplendent shone; my bridles golden-rein'd
And silver-bitted, while my lackeys wore
Regalia glittering with golden ore.

"Courted, caress'd and flatter'd by the fair.
　My bosom still felt no responsive throb,
But license only; I always had my share
　Of that elixir, with a thirst to rob.
Yet is not this good Anglo-Saxon taste,
Provided one who robs will also waste.

"I spent my days in adding to that pile
　That gave me leave to while away the night,
In private boxes, caressed with many a smile,
　Which seem'd to say, 'Perditus, you are right!
Make money: in all the catalogue of crime
Is none so great as being without a dime.'

" I had become the lion of the day,
    And truly felt I had achiev'd my end—
That my surmise as to the proper way
    Of judging mankind was right; I defend
This line of policy, which is all comprest
Into lie, cheat, steal, but avoid arrest.

" How soon will pa to darling daughter say,
    ' My child, your beau is quite a clever man,
And if he ask, pray do not answer nay,
    But if he won't, then make him if you can ;
That other lad, who keeps the corner store
Is honest, dear, but then, you know he's poor.'

" Geniuses were always fools, that is to say,
    Worshippers of aught outside of money,
Dwelling in dream-worlds, pass their lives away
    In poverty and want, while milk and honey
Flow in profusion at the feet of him
Without taste sufficient to relish them.

" This is the world—the greedy sordid world—
    I knew it well and read its lines aright,
Elbow'd my way through crowds, defiance hurl'd
    Upon opposing scamps, and made but light
Of their pretensions. Who car'd to know
Whom I had been when I was thriving so ?

" I am no worse than others—carried out
    What they have taught—let some men gnash their teeth ;
I found in youth that mankind prate about
    Dishonest gain, and yet contrive a wreath
For him who gains it. How this stubborn truth
    Does shock the soul of unsuspecting youth.

"I might, when young, have gone to books and made
    A name perhaps that future chroniclers
Had been proud to mention, but I surveyed
    The sons of genius oft in rags and tears,
And begging bread! I did not hesitate
As to my choice, and hence my better fate.

"But why philosophize? 'Tis known to all,
    Fame buys no luxury, but money will.
Wit, without doubt, to some extent by all
    Is a thing desir'd, yet it can never fill
A woman's eye, but diamonds often can,
In her opinion, make an ass a man.

"Now I had fix'd my lech'rous eyes upon
    A belle as fair as any in the town.
True, she had ask'd, and I had favors done,
    And for her sake I thrust my fingers down
Deep in my pockets; bought a house and lot
For her dear sake and took her to the spot.

"She was my mistress--none can be a swell
    Without at least some adjunct of this sort;
Must have a wife, whom he loves passing well,
    And yet another, whose dalliance and sport
Is far more pleasing to the vulgar heart
Than she whom good men call our 'better part.'

"Ere long I was the scandal of the city;
    Friends without number strove to intercede;
Tea-loving matrons averr'd it was a pity
    That I should leave my better half and lead
A life of shame; I, like a senseless brute,
    *   *   *   *   *   *   *

"I went too far, for vice expos'd is crime.
    Do as you please, but let not others know
Your secret sins: too soon avenging time
    Will do this for you. Some things none must know
Except yourself; fools only advertise
Their weaknesses, but never so the wise.

"I knew of love in youth, but what is love
    In woman's eye, except an empty dream
When one is poor? Your gentle, cooing dove,
    The sweetest coos, when she beholds the beam
Of opulence, and best reciprocates
When she can find no lien on your estates.

"I spent my days in one incessant round
    Of dissipation till I saw a corner
In stock, and then, indeed, I could be found
    With bulls and bears making banks a mourner.
I darken'd days with golden speculation,
And frighten'd even the credit of the nation.

"In summer time I hied me to the springs,
    Whereat to meet the most congenial snobs,
Where demoiselles and other costly things—
    Gamblers, *roues*, the urbane knave who robs
Three quarters of a year, contrive to meet,
To flaunt their gains and hold communion sweet.

"Were you e'er there? If not, by all means go,
    'Tis something to be seen well worth the sight;
All classes here eat fashionable crow,
    Not mincingly, but with a sheer delight;
Madame Vulgus here ascends to Madame Taste,
Provided she has gold enough to waste.

" From him who sits upon the highest seat
  That nations give e'en to the most obscure,
In this one spot may hold communion sweet:
  But one thing here, and that is to be poor,
Debars the pleasant interchange of talk,
And makes ' sweet Miss' decline to take a walk.

" Obsequious ushers bleed you like a leech,
  And porters charge a most enormous rate,
While ragamuffins crowd upon the beach,
  And run ahead to open every gate ;
And then demand in such a pesky way,
You are disgrac'd if you refuse to pay.

" Here congregate the odds and ends of life,
  The heads and tails of fashionable folly ;
Some rich, old fool, whose young and dashing wife
  Forgets her spouse, also her melancholy,
Flirts with her young and fashionable beau
And teaches him the art of eating crow.

" Some bogus lord breaks in upon the scene,
  Becomes at once the lion of the day ;
All Swelldom ceases for once to be serene,
  And native stars forget their wonted ray ;
But perturbation spreads throughout the camp,
When *ma belle* finds her lordship is a scamp.

" 'Tis after all a fashionable fair,
  Where ev'ry thing at least is brought to view
Except one thing, and that is, what you are ;
  This little trifle is not required of you.
Here men and women (pardon the expression)
Hold Folly's Court, for once, in open session.

" I did not lag, for ere this you have seen
    I am ambitious—falsely I confess—
But drove amain, convinced that I could lean
    Upon my money, and quite dispense *finesse.*
No need of wit, so long as money brings
Facetious fools to sell their funny things.

" It does require a superhuman nerve
    In such a place to stay the season out,
The whales alone can manage to preserve
    A steady front amid the gen'ral rout
Of smaller fishes, as the season ends
With empty pockets and exhausted friends.

OBITUARY OF PERDITUS.

Perditus is dead, a sly assassin's shot
    Cut down his life; the sequel of his fate
I herein give, *gratis*, but it is not
    My purpose at all to extenuate,
Nor drag to light from all their dark recesses,
His evil deeds, short-comings, and excesses.

A man he was, no doubt of able mind,
    Form'd to contrive and carry daring deeds,
His moral sense perverted wrong and blind,
    Yet flowers bloom amid the rankest weeds.
And rugged natures oft contain the gem
That far outweighs an outside diadem.

He was a type of those seen ev'ry day,
  Who never can a fair distinction draw
Twixt vice and virtue, wrong and proper way,
  License was liberty, tyranny, law.
He was no exception to the general rule
That sudden riches makes a man a fool.

Gen'rous, and yet without a sense of honor,
  Of courage deficient in moral sense,
Replete with tricks that only knaves would garner
  A cheat by nature, rogue without prepense;
The beau-ideal of a perfect man,
Made up expressly on the modern plan.

Accurs'd Society behold your son,
  The bold, bad man, who dar'd to carry out
What you have taught him. Do not seek to shun
  Your share in guilt, nor raise a hollow shout
Of indignation, for ye taught him first,
That of all crimes is poverty the worst.

Whate'er he was, call him no hypocrite,
  Such terms as this, at best befit him ill.
His darkest deeds were done in open light,
  And sought not he his purpose to instil,
By pleasing precepts, like a moral slave
Who would condemn indulgences they crave.

He sleeps at last, the greedy pack can yell
  And curses heap upon his harmless head.
Ornate divines construct his future hell.
  Asses can bray : they see the lion dead.
With God we leave him, He alone is just
And " knows our frame, and that we are but dust."
  II

Critical Poems.

THE MILLENIUM.

DEDICATED TO MY FRIEND, JOHN R. MABEN.

I.

ARGUMENT.

The law as contained in the Ten Commandments—Reflections of a general nature arising therefrom—The Gospel, General outline— Its after-history—The Patriarchs and other matters.

About four thousand years ago,
As Holy Writ and records show,
It pleas'd Almighty God to give
Ten legal rules by which to live,
Tho' for entire application,
Were given first to Jacob's nation,
Whom, in his wisdom, God had chose
To be his own, escap'd the throes
Of slavery and fled afar
From Egypt and her Potiphar.
For them the sea roll'd back its spray
On either side to give them way,
And scarce, as erst they touch'd the shore
Beyond, roll'd backward, as before,
Engulphing to the uttermost
The wicked King and all his host.
Yet this rebellious people broke
So oft the law of which we spoke

That God at length was forc'd to say,
"They shall not enter in but stay
In wilds and perish by the way."
It seems the veriest contradiction,
Yet Truth at times surpasses Fiction,
That God's elect would rather choose
To serve the Devil and refuse
The milk and honey, thus prefer
The leeks and onions to such cheer.
Yet so it is, and ever since
Mankind have shown a consistence
In this direction and upset
The best of methods known as yet,
For their own good, prefer perdition
To any Heaven " on condition,"
And reckon each succeeding Moses,
A knave that leads them by their noses.

SEQUENCE.

" Tall trees from little acorns grow,"
" And little drops make oceans flow,"
Were maxims taught us long ago,
And patent to the dullest mind,
That makes a study of its kind,
Is that *penchant* to magnify
What happen'd in an age gone by.
Take for example, if you please,
That story of Demosthenes,
Who, finding youthful words were rebels,
Subdued by pelting them with pebbles ;
And then, as if to recompense
Dame Nature for this grave offence,
Which Art had given, for his tones,
He spent his life in fear of stones.
'Tis well known that the human mind,
When idle will contrive to find

Some art or device to supply
The aching void and occupy
Itself, and serves it just as well,
A kingdom, or a bagatelle;
Thus we are told in Holy Writ
That Eve and Adam could not sit
'Neath Eden shades from day to day,
And pass celestial lives away;
But various are the ways that man
Invents to shun the hated ban
Of idleness; some guide the plow,
Some wield the pen, as we do now,
Some legislate, some preach and pray,   .
Do any thing—provide it pay:
And so it goes, and since the day
The law was given, some for pay,
And others love, have added to it,
That God himself would fail to know it.
And yet, as if to show its strength,
'Tis scatter'd thro' the breadth and length,
And bears the fruit, tho' sparsely sow'd,
Throughout each looming code,
Embellish'd with ten thousand rules,
That charm the wise and cheat the fools.

THE GOSPEL.

Some eighteen hundred years ago,
As Holy Writ and records show,
A child was born in Bethlehem
Of Judea, and Magi came
From Eastern parts to worship Him,
And bringing frankincense and myrrh,
Such gifts as Orients prefer.
The Wondrous Child became a man
Of wisdom full and then began
His Heav'nly purpose to fulfil,

Which was to do his Father's will.
The simple doctrines by him taught,
Were all with love and wisdom fraught—
"Love one another" was the key
To all of his theology,
Which was comprised, in greater part,
In loving God with all thy heart,
And soul and mind, this, just above,
"Thy neighbor as thy self to love."
At proper time twelve men he chose
From humble life and taught to those
By signs and wonders by him done,
He was the long expected One
Whom Prophets in the days of old
Did write about, and had foretold.
His purpose fill'd, he died for man
In accord with his Father's plan,
Yet ere corruption o'er him spread,
He rose victorious from the dead,
As David in the Psalms had said,
And went to Heaven, there to make
Full intercession for the sake
Of all that hate him, pointing to
The wounds inflicted by the Jew.
The Twelve were sent thro' all the earth
To tell the story of his birth,
And life, and death, and to proclaim
Salvation only thro' his name.
Some went to Athens, some were sent
To teach barbarians to repent,
With power giv'n from God-head
To heal the sick and raise the dead,
Result of which the truth was sown
In all the earth at that time known,
Which bore the fruits of blameless life,
Since peace they taught instead of strife.

Some fifty years, when they were dead,
A sudden quarrel overspread
All Christendom as to the Head
Of primal churches, and began
That "war of words" that puzzles man,
As he the simple story reads
And then compares it with the creeds
That flood the earth and crowd the shelves
With explanations of—themselves.

SPECULATIONS.

Some writer says, (dispute who can,)
The study chief of man is man.
The theme no doubt affords a field
Immense to such as love to wield
Their talents in a varied way,
"Severe and lively, grave and gay."
Perhaps a few examples here
Will serve to make the subject clear:
One, in a religious light,
Inspects his subject day and night,
And striking on some happy hint,
A volume rushes into print,
Replete with reasoning prodigious,
To prove that mankind is religious;
Others, of philosophic bent,
Regard him as a monument
Unfinish'd still; the only price
Requir'd now is their advice
Contain'd in calves, that on the shelves
Resemble monuments themselves.
Others, in a social way,
Ransack the past, the "good old day,"
And reason, as a thing of course,
The fount is purer at its source,
Go back unto the very day

Our parents sinn'd and fell away,
Beholds them losing Eden's bliss,
Their talents turn to mending this,
Reviews the honest Patriarchs,
Ere paving streets and grading parks
Had come in use or been in vogue
To starve the poor, enrich the rogue,
No money to appropriate
For thieving rings to speculate,
When mankind were too pure to breed
A slippery Dick or Oily Tweed,
When strict *patersfamilias*
Engross'd their bills and let them pass,
When tents were capitals and when
No lawyer had appear'd to men,
With points and disquisitions nice,
And heavy fees for light advice;
No Congress then to legislate,
Enacting laws to rob the State;
No "salary grabs," no subsidies,
No long debates defending these;
Each individual family
Believ'd in "squatter sovereignty,"
Without ransacking books and shelves,
Enacted laws to suit themselves.
Ah, "Little Giant!" piteous fate,
To live five thousand years too late,
Yet this alas, is oft the case,
Right men are born in the wrong place;
Or, to set the sense more clearly,
Either born too late or early,
And miss by chance, or accident,
A gibbet or a monument:
More simple still the married state
Existing at that early date,
For facts do not substantiate,

That Parsons at that day existed,
By whom the nuptial knot was twisted ;
No need of thirds, as moderns do,
In matters which concern but two ;
No courtship and no empty vows,
But "will you milk my goats and cows?"
If answer'd "yes," at once they went—
Not to the Parson, but the tent,
And for the balance of her life
No *femme converte*, but trusting wife.
To make it yet more simple still
Oft times a servant could fulfil
The trust, while modern times require
All kith and kin, as well as sire
To bring about, and then a dozen
Left angry, with their "loving cousin,"
At being married in a trice,
Without obtaining their "advice ;"
Whilst oily parsons consecrate
The dainty dish in pompous state,
And smelling much of books and shelves,
Occasion take to air themselves,
Pronounces them as duly wed,
Tho' neither heard the half he said,
Obtains a kiss, and then his fee ;
No further need of such as he.

Exhaustless subject, you can see
Without addition, therefore we,
To see what men say of themselves,
Have but to search the stalls and shelves
Throughout the land, and we shall find
A number written in this kind :
"It may be noted at a glance,
Complexity means an advance,"
Says one, " from all established rules,

Adopted both to wise and fools,
Whereas it takes a lifetime now
To know not why man lives, but how ;"
Therefore this one doth contend
Simplicity is the chief end
Of government, and boldly says:
"A state of Nature is the phase
That God intended." This *sans doute*
Might suit an angel or a brute.
Enough of nonsense; vain to quote
What fools conceived or dunces wrote.
Back to the text, we only meant
To speak of an experiment,
And therefore without more ado,
We bring it to the reader's view.

II.

The Discovery of Utopia—The Country Described—Character of the Natives—The Emigrants who settled it—Some Facts in its History Thereafter.

Time out of mind it has been taught,
That human nature could be brought
To full perfection by some plan
Submitted not by God, but man ;
So in accordance with this scheme,
Which tallies with the poet's dream,
And adds immense *eclat* and glory,
To certain styles of oratory ;
Great Plato first on fancy drew
For ideal kingdoms, which if true
And practical, had been no doubt,
The same enthusiasts prate about,
Yet failing, deem not Plato's plan,
Will ever lose its weight with man,
For scores of sages yet will say,

"The fault was but in Plato's day,
When half the world in darkness lay.
Could he have had our modern aids
And helps to reconcile the shades
Of diff'rence in the common mind
And such discrepancies as find
Themselves in systems newly tried,
Plato had seen it ere he died;*
Had seen a people in whose law
No expert could detect a flaw—
"The best that mankind ever saw."
The last assertion seems to lead
To explanations; we proceed
To give it without more ado
Than's necessary thereunto.

THE DISCOVERY.

Remote from other worlds was found
A country vast and richly crowned
With all that Natures' lavish hand
Could ever give, or God command.
Interminable forests stood,
Abounding in all kinds of wood,
The poplar's tall majestic head
In vallies rich its branches spread,
The various species of the oak
With giant arms outspreading spoke,
A fertile soil whereon it grew
To size immense, the solemn yew
Entwin'd, as bridegroom doth the bride,
The waving cypress at its side,
The fields bedeck'd with ev'ry fruit
Sweet to the taste of of man or brute,
The apple and delicious peach
Weighed down the laden limbs in reach,
As if inviting man to try

Their sweetness as he passes by ;
In clusters hung the juicy grape
On vines of wild fantastic shape,
That clung to some supporting tree
Like Virtue does to Chastity.
The fields were redolent with sweets
Of flowers wild, whose wide retreats
Were not pent up by wall or glass,
But free to all to pluck who pass,
Rare birds of ev'ry hue and note
The ravish'd ear with music smote ;
In forests stalked the agile deer,
The grizzly bear that hunters fear ;
Broad rivers pour'd their rapid spray
Thro' vallies vast to pass away
In gulfs, whose great immensity
Assumed proportions of a sea.

THE NATIVES.

But stranger still, this goodly land,
As if on purpose had been planned
For gods themselves, was peopled then
With a peculiar race of men,
Whose origin must still remain
A mystery since none explain,
Yet this is certain, none deny,
This goodly land that charmed the eye
Was their's alone—this by the way—
Yet more concerning such as they.

THE SETTLEMENT.

Hail, Mighty Era! which consigned
Another world, wherein mankind,
In what the Old had fail'd to do,
Might now accomplish in the New ;
For what are all new worlds intended,

Except like old ones, to be mended;
But mark you, note the varied range
Of ideas which the sudden change
This new and great discovery wrought
In all the realms of human thought!
The grasping miser dream'd at night
Of golden bars and rubies bright,
Adventurous souls beheld a field
Which they at once could force to yield
Excitements, which could satisfy
The need that well known haunts deny,
The man of fame at once gave way
To mighty dreams of regal sway.
'Tis true no formidable foe
Confronted him with battle's show,
But wild and undisciplin'd race,
Who liv'd by hunting and the chase,
And yet success is all the same
If that your foe be wild or tame,
Provided seas but roll between
And you the Hero of the scene—
Example, "Cæsar's Commentaries:"
How widely from the truth it varies;
None can determine since the Gaul,
To contradict, left none at all.
"Enchantment" not alone to mounts
Doth distance lend, but fierce accounts
Of bloody battles never fought,
And deeds of daring never wrought.
'Tis useless to suspect a lie
Without the proof to verify,
Or, *au contraire*, believe forsooth
A man who never tells the truth.
Thus wisely thought the man of fame,
Of all such things before he came.
The good religions divined

His mission was to leave behind
A people whom the gospel leaven
Prepar'd sufficiently for Heaven,
And go 'mongst savages to preach
New ways of life, also to teach
A blind belief in wornout creeds,
(Yet always new to one who needs,)
In well-authenticated deeds
Of saints, whose history so twisted
'Tis doubtful if the same existed,
Yet if they did, and still exist
Around us now, as some insist,
They spend their time to solve the mystery
Of finding themselves writ in history.
Such *credos* and a thousand others
Felt call'd to teach benighted brothers,
And, who in case of non-compliance
With his desire, or worse, defiance
Of Gospel law, and thus upset
The rules of Christian etiquette,
And of such rules the very chief
Is an implicit, blind belief
In tales so near akin to fiction,
They carry their own contradiction.
And if thus the savage mind,
Tho' to the marvelous inclin'd,
Refuses fictions of this kind,
And clings to gods of wood and stone,
Rather than search for One Unknown,
Why, in this case, of course the church
Would never leave him in the lurch;
Moreover, to insure success,
Would make the earth one savage less,
That is, prefer the lesser evil
Of sending *one* to see the Devil
To losing *all*—the logic see

I

In this, oh pious devotee!
But this discovery was god-send
To those whose time and talents tend
In every age to fabricate
Perfection for the human state,
Who, failing of success, lament
The lack of an experiment
Wherein theories suggested,
By themselves, be tried and tested.
And here it was a chance for once
For ev'ry theoretic dunce
To show his hand and try his skill,
And all his prophecies fulfill.
Then came a heterogeneous mass
Of mankind, forming ev'ry class
Existing at that early day,
To fell the woods and clear the way.
The knave and saintly Puritan,
The liar, thief and courtesan,
Highwayman, (title dignified
With that of chieftain,) came in pride
Of place and power to assume
All honors him denied at home;
The buccaneer on booty bent,
The pious missionary sent
To teach young heathens to repent;
Artificer and artisan
Came out in crowds or busy clan,
With royal rakes despis'd at Court,
" Lewd fellows of the baser sort "
Who gen'rously their presence lent
To swell the grand experiment,
And thus Utopia became
Inhabited by all the lame
And blind and halt, who hitherto
Had been at home with naught to do,

Except to live at the expense
Of others in their indigence.
Beyond a doubt such crowds before
Had never flock'd to any shore,
And what befel them, what their fate,
We circumspectly now relate:
We had forgot before to name,
In specifying such as came
To see Utopia, that they
No idea had thro' life to stay;
Result of which each one desired
A fame or fortune well acquired,
Would then forsake the foreign shore
And ne'er return to plague it more;
Result, that others bent on theft
Supplied the place of such as left.
These, in their turn, also gave way
To other gangs still bent on prey.
How long such practices as those
Might have continued no one knows,
Had competition not prevented
This evil practice, and cemented
The predatory bands, to stay
And watch their rivals by the way;
For mark you, soon as it was known
All nations claim'd it as their own:
There hither came in motley groups,
Not only emigrants but troops,
And these, right naturally, fell out;
But this we need not write about,
Suffice to say, amongst the rest,
There came a band whose ranks possest
A genuine philosopher,
Whose history is given here:—

III

*Contains an account of a Philosopher whose theories were adopted
concerning Utopia—An Elephant is Introduced in the Colony—
His History is given, and the Millenium dawns.*

"About three hundred years ago,
When bread was high and pay was low,
When one could scarcely earn by labor
Enough to entertain a neighbor,
There sprung in these remoter ages
One of the wisest of the sages,
Who ever went upon a trail,
To shoot a deer or trap a quail.
We have been told by those who knew,
He was as kind as he was true,
And fed the poor upon the border,
Who had no means to purchase powder;
For without this no one could buy
Enough of meat to make a fry,
For in that day, as well as this,
One's meat and bread ne'er came amiss.
Nor science, literature and learning,
A stomach ne'er kept from yearning.
And what is found most necessary
To learning is a commissary;
And eloquence is mostly found
Where beef is cheapest in the pound,
While wit and wine, all mortals know,
Invariably together flow.
Well, this Philosopher got tired
Of being in this way admired,
For soon he found it would not bring
Along with it the needful thing;
For fame is but a mere gewgaw
To one who has an empty maw:
Tho' it entitle to the skies,

No one's so bent to win the prize,
As set out with an empty belly
To run the risk of cake and jelly.
A sudden change at once was wrought
In this old Philosopher's thought;
No more content to trap the deer,
Or hear his rifle ringing clear;
Another thought supplied him food,
Than hero of his neighborhood.
By some contrivance he had found
The earth not square, but nearly round,
And yet his neighbors all would swear
He ever acted "on the square."
This was the difference, as you see,
Twixt practice and his theory.
From one extreme into another
He ran, since he could run no further,
Ceas'd talking of antipodes,
Of burning zones and polar seas.
Political economy
At once employ'd him, yet he
No treatise ever read or saw
But intuition gave him law;
Like many others, had, he said,
"The Wealth of Nations in his head."
This led him into speculation,
Not for himself but for the nation,
And sooth to say this latter spirit,
His pushing offspring all inherit;
Prefer to manage all affairs
Except their own, nay run on shares
The world itself, provided they,
In common parlance, "make it pay."

Our Solon saw, with much distress,
The land a howling wilderness;

So he bethought him how to get
The labor that it needed yet,
Not e'en Hectors and Ajaxes,
He deem'd, could fell the trees with axes:
Therefore this plan he recommended
How trees might both be cut and rended.
By putting powder 'neath their trunks
And blowing them at once to chunks.
So, like all other innovators,
He tried, the first, his apparatus.
A white oak large before his door,
In height some fifty feet or more,
Whose trunk, when measu'd at its base,
Some dozen feet or more or less.
Beneath its trunk he dug a hole,
And in it did a barrel roll
All laden to the brim with powder,
Enough to blow the tree to chowder,
Next pour'd his fuse along the ground.
Applied a match and made a bound
Within his hut and shuts the door,
Stops up his ears and waits the roar,
As if two worlds had come together,
Whose purpose was to crush each other.
Was that report that seem'd to shake
The pillars of this globe opaque;
One limb was thrown against the door,
And knock'd him sprawling on the floor.
Another on his roof was blown
And madly kick'd his chimney down,
And when at length the Solon woke
He found his cabin full of smoke,
And rushing out, at once he saw,
A scene of ruin and of awe;
For all the trees, for yards around,
Were pil'd and scatter'd on the ground.

A week it took him, labor hard,
To get the rubbish from his yard,
And then it took a week or more,
To get his house as 'twas before.
As to his plans of felling trees
You might have thought would stop with these:
But other schemes were in his head,
Ere he of this had trial made.
Thus genius never can be spent
Save thro' its own, its native bent.
Water never runs up hill;
But genius does, and ever will;
One yields to force of nature blind;
The other to the laws of mind,
For genius craves and must inherit
The higher altitudes of spirit.

THE NEW IDEA.

On Afric's coast, he had been told,
That elephants were bought and sold,
Whose trunks also contain'd the key
To much of labor's mystery;
Yet, as his wealth would not suffice
To purchase them at present price,
He laid the scheme before his neighbors,
How they could mitigate their labors.
And sooth to say, they all agreed,
That elephants would stand their need.
Therefore on all he made a levy,
Enough to buy a cargo heavy,
And then he hasten'd to the coast,
Where Spanish traders frequent most,
And made at once a stipulation
Not for himself, but for the nation:
And whilst the trader sought the coast
Of Africa, at home they boast.

" How soon the trees would disappear,
When we receive our cargo here;"
They thought the elephantine snout
Could pull up trees and drag them out.
At length the mighty cargo came
Of elephants both wild and tame.
It seem'd at first the scheme would pay:
Experience drove such hopes away;
The climate was too cold and bleak,
The elephants grew lean and weak.
What should they do? Not send them back
To roam again their native track!
Oh, no; that scheme would never pay,
Appear however good it may,
Their charity directs itself
In paths alone producing pelf.
"Necessity can have no law"
Was utter'd by some luckless "saw,"
Who found himself within a place,
Which had no outlet but disgrace,
And us'd it as a valid plea
To get out of his villainy.
If right and wrong can have no meaning,
If they are but the idle gleaning
Of men whose smooth and easy fate
Was never put to such a strait,
Then may we use it in the day
When honesty has ceas'd to pay.
Some witty fellow tells us too,
(We only wonder how he knew,)
She is the mother invention
And other things we may not mention.
Well, if a time had ever been
That call'd for all the wit of men,
That time was this, to free the nation
From this animal creation.

The good philosopher was dead,
Who put this idea in their head,
And if he now had been about,
Would found that time had put it out,
But these brethren did inherit
A part of his inventive spirit.
At once they quickly turn'd about
And found a way to get them out;
They shipp'd them almost in a trice,
And sold them off at any price.
What next? for verily it seems
Their meat and drink consist of schemes
Of self-advancement, while pretending
Another's right to be defending, ·
Turn all christianity to pelf
And traffic make in prayer itself.
All this, with many other things,
To notice, the next chapter brings.

IV.

The Dawn of the Millenium—Some Clouds that Obscured the Glories of its Rising Sun—The Elephant a Stumbling Block—Conflicting Views as to the Best Manner of Disposing of Him—After Much Contention he is Admitted into the Human Family—The Age of Philosophers who are to bring about the consummation of all things—The Battle of the Armageddon, ect., conclude the chapter.

It happen'd in the course of Time,
Not Pollok's,—that is too sublime;
For our purpose, in this place,
Deals not at all with human race,
How man is sav'd or how he's lost,
But chief concerns that mighty host
Of elephants, both wild and tame,
Whom we have told from Afric came;
Let us, in short, reiterate

That Chapter Second did relate
To a unique and novel trade
The Modern *Saints* with Sinners made.
In this it is propos'd to tell
What to these elephants befell
In that more congenial place,
The home of all the dusky race;
And therefore without more ado
The history is brought to view.
'Tis well known animal creation,
Like man, has power of propagation,
Like him in many other senses,
Without regard to consequences,
Therefore the same, as human species,
Became as numerous as fishes;
But still their owners found a way
To make the dusky creatures pay,
For those who purchas'd them and bought,
Were beings of another sort,
And quickly, readily they found,
These elephants could till the ground;
Found him, besides to be withal,
Well treated, a good animal,
In consequence the people grew
Immensely rich, as would ensue
To all who mind their own affairs,
And let not others trouble theirs.

SAINTLY JEALOUSY.

The Devil's work-shop, it is said,
Is found in ev'ry idler's head.
No doubt Old Nick there often dwells
And makes a thousand little hells
Of petty spites and jealousies,
Of envy at another's ease:
Indeed, no sore was ever found

Like that immedicable wound,
Inflicted when a hated rival
Contrives to rise by no contrival,
Or help of ours, overleaping
The bounds we set for his safe keeping.
Thus was it, as the sequel shows,
With those who bought and traded those
Gigantic animals, which found
No sustenance on saintly ground,
Had found them, tho' they would not pay,
Their equals almost ev'ry way:
Next came a philosophic race
Of saints, with powers full to trace
The source of ev'ry ill or good
Afflicting mankind since the flood,
In each succeeding system saw
The want of one prevailing law;
Who saw as (if by intuition)
All that belong'd to man's condition.
They soon began to agitate
On what they term'd the "social state,"
And next to prove (behold the sequel)
That all things were created equal,
And fill'd the earth with wind and rant
(Sandwiched with due amount of cant)
And all about an elephant.
Meanwhile said elephant, content,
Perform'd the task that he was sent.
And never dreamt the world without,
Was getting into grief about
Himself. 'Twas pity thrown away :
Oh, no; have they not made it pay !

THE ELEPHANT AFORETIME—THE SINNERS AND SAINTS CON-
TRASTED, ETC.

Oft where the Nile, or Niger flows
Tho' sunny wastes, and brightly throws

The gleaming sunlight from his breast,
His memory at times in quest
Of some dear object, deign'd to go,
But where it was he did not know.
He saw the dark and dismal day,
When he was seiz'd and brought away,
Then of the deep and rolling sea,
Ne'er seen before by such as he,
Then of the cold and sterile soil,
Where he was first inur'd to toil,
Then of the cold relentless snow,
The bitter piercing winds that blow
Remorseless thro' its winters' long,
Where ev'n birds refuse a song;
Now in a hospitable clime,
Where all the year was summer time;
The lark and linnet sweetly sung,
The field and farm with music rung;
Where to the music of banjo
They "tripp'd the light fantastic toe."

THE SINNERS.

But, best of all, their masters were
The keepers they could love and fear,
No prating fools who went around,
To fill the earth with empty sound;
No vowing that their souls would melt
With pity they had never felt,
No turning systems inside out,
No social surgeons mad to flout
Their placards in the face of men,
No more commandments than the "Ten;"
An air of noble *neglige*
Appears in all they do or say,
No cold and philosophic breed
Dispensing virtues that they need.

A daring and impetuous race
Imbued with hunting and the chase,
By nature prone to ridicule
The cant of Puritanic school,
Or trash of transcendental fool, ·
No straight-laced ministers, whose shelves
Preach Hell to all except themselves.

THE SAINTS.

But volumes it would take to mention
About that nation of invention
Whose long alliterative phrase
Crops out in all it writes and says,
For since *Pere* Adam first began
To people this wide world with man,
There never has before existed
A people so perverse and twisted,
With traits and humors all so blended,
No man can tell whence they descended:
Red, blue, and black (in chief the latter)
Seem mingled in their moral platter;
Ev'n they themselves refuse to lick
The plate that makes all others sick,
All things in Heaven, Earth, or Hell,
Serve equally their purpose well.
We have been told their first appearance
Upon this earth was interference
With things establish'd long ago,
And which they tried to overthrow,
But in their turn were driv'n out
For being rather too devout.
Their deep abhorrence, too, of witches,
Of luxury and handsome breeches;
Their gloomy love and sour looks,
Their deep antipathies to books,
Save of the heavy, solemn kind

J

That treat of all to Hell consigned,
Except themselves; their moral law,
Worse than Egyptian "bricks and straw;"
Their solemn, sanctimonious airs,
Their fondness for the longest prayers;
The rueful cant and nasal twang,
In which they either spoke or sang;
Their blue laws and their peace conventions,
Their sour pride and high pretensions
To sanctity, the very traces
The Devil wrote upon their faces,
So twisted, as to say and mean,
"See what a Saint I must have been!"
Their utter want of toleration,
And woful lack of veneration;
Their impudence and self-conceit
Strike ev'ry one they chance to meet,
In Senate, forum, or the street:
These be who sing "Millenium,"
And bring about the "Kingdom Come."

PHILOSOPHERS AMONG THE SAINTS.

Next came a philosophic race,
With full abilities to trace
The source of ev'ry ill or good
Afflicting mankind since the flood.
These deep philosophers were given
To speculate on earth, as Heaven;
Saw universal law pervading
The paths to Heaven they were grading;
Saw all kindreds, peoples, tongues
Mix, and Nature do no wrong;
Saw all prejudice and passion,
Of natures foreign in compassion;
Saw white and smutty Hottentot
All boiling in a common pot,

And, what one never read in fable,
All eating at a common table;
Saw Dutchman and his *liebe bier*
Embrace, then part for water clear;
Valet de chambre and queenly marin
Together walking arm in arm;
Saw mistress and her slutty maid,
The genius and the worthless jade
All on a level and a grade:
Hence, gentle reader, do not doubt
Aught impossible without
Some sudden freak shall mar the plan
They'll prove that man is more than man,
And that in time the brute creation
Will occupy his former station.
Invention, endless at its source,
God only knows their next recourse.
In truth then to this maxim heed,
They never do a dirty deed
Of wickedness, but that they plead
Philanthropy, while devils laugh
To see mankind seduced with chaff.

THE DOCTORS OF THE NEW DIVINITY.

The laws of Nature are defined
Quite similar to those of Mind:
That is to say, in each we see
An equal inequality.
The river mingles with the main,
Rills make the rivers o'er again,
The great at last absorbs the small,
Short trees must grow beneath the tall,
Or else they cannot grow at all,
Some lofty, solitary peak,
Absorbs the mount the eye would seek,
Superior mind must have its sway,

The lesser must of course obey,
And its full tithe of homage pay :
Still more, absurd as it may seem,
One must in folly reign supreme,
So that in both, as one can see,
Remains an inequality ;
And who, therefore, denies this rule,
Is neither more nor less than fool.
But now a period had arrived
When Wisdom fail'd and Folly thrived,
When all dictates of common sense
Were thrown aside without pretense,
And doctrines that could never suit
Man, angel, animal or brute,
Were taught by dunce or *doctrinaire*
With explanations to a hair.
Th'infection spread from sire to son,
From head to foot, till all were one,
Whilst converts to the New Idea
Soon spread from Dan to Bersheba.
Now came the full millenial hour
When all the Saints should be in power,
St. Carlos, leading in the van,
Loom'd up forthwith the "coming man,"
By nature blest with a physique
That all men covet, women seek,
A pair of lungs that could emit
A windy volume, but no wit,
A head so fashion'd as contain
All other things except a brain,
Of whom, in truth, it can be said,
Had but one idea in his head,
And that was wrong, and yet by might
Of long orations, made it right,
Of knowledge great and wisdom small,
A pile without a spark at all,

Who in the drag-net of his mind,
Could ideas take but of one kind,
An educated weather-cock,
Of fools, the leader of the flock,
Stark mad, with ideas just as wild
As ever fill'd the head of child.
Honest indeed was he, no doubt,
Fanatics are, or just about ;
Forgiving, sooth, he died of late
And left his "legacy of hate."
St. Horace next, in differ'nt sphere,
Was more than equal and compeer :
A writer, orator and sage,
One who could sprinkle on his page
More wit than Carlos in an age ;
Eccentric Saint, and yet withal
"The noblest Roman of them all,"
Who, when provok'd, could fiercely cry
"You lie, you villain ; you know you lie!"
St. Phillips, greatest of them all
To rouse, excite and stir up gall,
The Boauerges, from whose mouth
Both wit and madness issued forth.
The incarnation of the Devil
In rousing men to deeds of evil,
Yet after all, as facts have shown,
Like others, fights by wind alone ;
His voice, like a trumpets tongue,
To panting crowds "the changes rung"
In burning words that smote at once
Through cranium of the thickest dunce.
These be the chief, tho' others bear
In labor, like an equal share.

THE BATTLE OF THE ARMAGEDDON, WHICH BRINGS THIS HIS-
TORY TO THE EVE OF MILLENIUM.

'Tis good to recapitulate
At times, in other words, to state
What has been written once before,
For explanations sake—no more.
Be it remember'd then a trade,
Concerning elephants, was made
'Twixt Saint and Sinner, and wherein
The Saint's abhorrence of the sin
Of elephantine slavery
Occurs not in this knavery.
In course of time, some way or other,
They learn'd to love them as a brother;
Nay, found them, tho' they would not pay,
Their equals fully ev'ry way.
Experience proves beyond a doubt
That that was true, nay carries out,
That elephants, in honesty,
Were their *superiors*, we shall see:
The bargain struck, at once began
A war of words that puzzles man;
Each lesser Saint to greater bowed
Horse, foot, dragoon—a motly crowd,
Till all Utopia became
Confusion worse than a Bedlam.
Ye gods! how wind and thunder roll'd
From such as lately bought and sold!
With what poetic frenzy told,
How elephants, from day to day,
In sighs and tears, groan'd life away!
At times the saintly bilingsgate
Was measureless; invoking Fate,
And all the furies out of Hell,
Forthwith to come the curse to quell;
Pronounced the writ that gave them breath,

" A league and covenant with death ! "
Like saints, who true Millenium saw,
Began to preach "the higher law,"
In short, to ruin fabric reared
By patriots whom worlds revered,
For that alone which only time,
And that, but short, to prove a crime,
Which public sentiment would damn,
Without recourse to cant and sham.
Yet those who owned them calmly stood,
With patience long ago subdued,
In hopes at least a better mind
Might seize a populace so blind,
Great souls there were on either side
Who sought to stem the fearful tide:
One who in prophetic awe,
His country's degradation saw,
And warn'd them of their coming fate,
His sole reward—his country's hate.
Another pray'd the beauteous sun,
Whose beams he last might gaze upon,
Might never shine upon a State
Drench'd in fraternal blood, but fate
Took his capacious soul away
Before the horrors of that day.
It came—alas, the dreadful day !
A million homes in ruin lay
As fire and sword in fury swept
O'er fields that late in harvests slept,
And sow'd the earth above, beneath,
With Hell's own idea—dragon's teeth.
'Tis past—the elephant is free,
His master slave instead of he.

V.

The Millenium in Full Blast—A Great Change Overcomes All Utopia Save One—Great Gathering of the Saints at the New Jerusalem—Two New Saints are Created and Admitted into the Happy Family—Ere long a War Breaks Out in the Holy City— The Original Saints Overcome by New Converts and Thrown Out—Alarming Rumors Fill the Air—The Explosion, and Return to Common Sense.

Now had arriv'd the wond'rous age
That brought Millenium on the stage,
The consummation of all things,
When servants, boot-blacks, queens and kings,
When Saturn, Jupiters and Mars,
Nor more nor less than little stars.
Behold also the wondrous change
In Nature's universal range!
The nice gradations disallowed,
That God design'd, in jumbles crowd
Upon each other; tar became
Molasses, infamy was fame;
Salt turned to sugar, black and white
Were all the same, and darkness light:
The ass by right divine became
The genius; the wild was tame,
And, *vice versa*, dunces grew
To parts surpassing Richelieu;
Base imitation turned to Art,—
The whole but equal to a part.
And woman, spite of Heaven's plan,
Strove by enactment to be man,
And prov'd that modesty and sense
Were now in the pluperfect tense;
Poetasters, (no misnomer)
To Miltons turn'd or else a Homer.
The daubing dunce with master-piece

Outshone Appelles, Son of Greece;
The crazy bawler in the street,
Of wind chock full and self-conceit,
Was reckon'd could not fall below
Demosthenes or Cicero,
The empty-headed statesman hit
Above the mark of William Pitt,
The lawyer small of county court
Became an Erskine, and in short,
The low buffoon and clever wit
Shook hands across " the bloody pit ;"
Religion, for salvation sent,
Became a cloak or ornament,
Thieves turn'd to saints and rogues became
As honest men ; the sense of shame
Was blotted out. How could mankind
Be perfect and be still confined
By any rule or precedent
God, man, or angel could invent ?
In fact all such were set aside,
And in their places new ones tried.
Now certain in Utopia
Refus'd to adopt the New Idea,
And still believ'd, as they were taught,
God made the world just as He ought,
That no suggestion, at its birth,
Of theirs, would have improv'd its worth,
Still thought, all threats to the contrary,
That he was right, and would not vary.

THE GATHERING OF THE SAINTS AT THE NEW JERUSALEM.

How sweet a sight it is to see
All brethren dwell in unity,
And when our own souls overflow
With mirth or joy, or grief or woe,
How sweet to make another feel

Just as we do in woe or weal!
With this high purpose well defined
And settled in the saintly mind,
It was resolv'd at once to meet
In conclave full and there complete
The ideal destiny of man
In full accordance with their plan.
St. Carlos first in power shone,
(Although St. Andrew held the throne)
For he, by speeches and complaints,
Became the leader of the Saints,
And tho' he lack'd the smallest gifts
Of leadership, yet by make-shifts
Which he had learn'd as theorizer,
Became some sort an organizer;
Beyond all this he had the force
Of earnestness, and this, of course,
Outweigh'd all brilliancy which man
May have without specific plan.
May God forbid that I should tear
One feather from his cap, so rare
Are honest men, for this he prov'd
By giving life to what he lov'd,
And to his very death believed
Himself Millenium had achieved.
No wonder then with some disdain
He frown'd on upstarts as they deign
To intimate an equal share
In glory, which he could not spare,
Yet while he nurs'd his sullen wrath,
The others barricade his path,
And in an unexpected hour
Deprive him both of place and power.
St. Simon old, and Oliver
Usurped the place of Carlos dear,
St. Henry in perfection bloomed

Whence Sinner Daniel was entombed,
St. Thaddeus appear'd in flames
Above the last of Sinner James;
But one alone could dare to vie
With him, and it was St. Cock-Eye;
St. John, whose record in the West
In years by gone was not the best,
In almost equal splendor shone
With any Saint so far made known,
St. William with his little bell,
Consigning Copperheads to Hell,
Or Heaven, as the case may be,
No matter which to such as he,
Had first laid hands on horns of bull,
"In conflict irrepressible;"
Sly Saint withal, that some thought he
Was not more statesman than a flea,
Who on the body politic
Could dodge, escape, or hide, or stick.

A WAR BREAKS OUT IN THE HOLY CITY.

Let dogs delight to bark and bite,
Let Sinners,—Saints must never fight
Except their common foe, the Devil;
For more than this will come of evil,
For if the Saints should disagree
And smite each, how shall we,
That is to say Sinners, decide
Which is the right or the wrong side?
But, notwithstanding, strife began
In New Jerusalem, and ran
From mouth to mouth till it became
A saintly scandal and a shame.
How it began behooves to tell,
For in it Saints arose and fell;
Well, then, without more surmise,

Began and ended in this wise:
St. Andrew, seeing a good cause,
Rebelled against the saintly laws,
Turn'd tale and fell, oh woful case!
Like Lucifer, at once from grace.
The consternation at his fall
Was universal; had the ball
The Saints inhabit split asunder,
Not more had been their fear or wonder.
Then came the fiercely blinded rage,
Which only Saints of any age,
Have ever felt, the force that lends
Hell's fury to the worst of fiends,
Religious bigot or fanatic,
Or other madmen, so erratic,
When foil'd in some hallucination,
Their own pet project, or creation.
Yet truth be said, " revenge is sweet,"
As much to human hearts that beat
Beneath a surplice, as elsewhere,
With this exception, God must share
In all its glory, since no blame
Must stick to deeds done in his name.
These modern Saints with one accord
Call'd first upon the Sovereign Lord,
Then fell to work with all the vim
Of devil (pardon) cherubim,
St. A. in motion set the ball,
St. George soon seconded the call;
This last imagin'd "in the sky
He saw a hole," but St. Cock-Eye,
Did soon convince him, that instead
Of sky, the hole was in his head,
And then by force of nature bent,
Ahead of all the rest he went
And prov'd to all beyond a doubt,

St. Andrew must needs be kick'd out.
Warm wax'd debate until it grew
Not only fast, but furious too,
Yet ev'ry sinner to a man,
Who happen'd in that Saintly clan,
Stood up for Andrew till the plan
Of good St. A. had come to grief,
By Sinner Andrew standing chief,
A short time only, when he went
From power, privileged to vent
. His spleen, in private life and ease,
And curse and damn St. Ulysses.

TWO NEW SAINTS APPEAR—AND THE REIGN OF THE SAINTS ON EARTH.

The Saints, tho' feeling quite secure
In pow'r and place, as yet were sore,
At heretics, once nam'd before,
Who still believed, all they could do
These Saints were men, tho' it is true
Has never seen the like before,
Nor God's will, wish'd to see them more.
The Saints, however cast about
How to convert or get them out;
Let none infer our intents evil,
In saying Saints oft need the Devil.
Are we not told in Holy Writ,
That "Nick" tried Job to prove his grit;
That virtue is not worth a pin,
Which never has rejected sin,
And troops none dare in action call
Are equal—just to none at all.
Not in this sense do we intend
To show our Saints right in the end,
But more to show how sin sometimes,
By proper use, condones its crimes,

K

And that to Saints access is given
To Hell sometimes as well as Heaven,
And that at times e'en Beelzebub
To Saints distress'd will throw a tub.

Well, be it so, the Saints began,
With microscopic eyes to scan
Their ranks, to choose a proper man
To undertake the dang'rous mission
Of bringing sinners to condition.
'Twas then the genius of Cock-Eye
Triumphant shone and flam'd on high,
That ev'ry eye upon the spot
Left him to cut the Gordian knot,
Tho' never he the credit got.
St. Cock-Eye did a thing or two,
Beyond what others ever knew,
Who trod the plain and dusty way,
Of dull routine, and would not stray,
He knew that over-anxious Saints
Would never vex him with complaints,
Nor that if he succeeded well,
If came his agents out of Hell;
And so by means so intricate,
That Hell or he alone could state,
He brought about an interview
With Beelzebub in order to
See if his master could supply
His need in this emergency.
St. Cock-Eye told him of the strait
The Saints were in, how very great
The danger was; how far and near
They sought for some bold volunteer
To face the music, that is teach
The New Jerusalem and preach
The Kingdom Come, whose very zeal

Might also cover what they steal.
Quoth Beelzebub, "in my domain,
O'er which I absolutely reign,
Is one whose spirit at beginning
Consign'd to me for heinous sinning,
And whose allotted punishment
Is that his spirit still be sent
Continually to Earth to fill
The heart of all his offspring still ;
'Tis he ' whose base ignoble blood
Has crept thro' scoundrels since the flood,'
The same that in Messiah's day
In Judas dwelt and did betray
His Master for the paltry pay
Of thirty pieces ; thro' all time
His name synonymous with crime,
Traitor, liar, pimp and knave,
Robber, villian, hound and slave,
Incapable of ever knowing
A better life, but ever growing
In wickedness, and must, per force,
Until the Judgment Day of course."
St. Cock-Eye quoth, "Great Master, tell
The name of this great Son of Hell,
By your account, at once I see,
This is the very *thing* for me ?"
"His name, my Son, is Scalawag,
His Cousin first, is Carpet-Bag,
And from the way they work together,
You will conclude love one another."
The bargain struck, St. Cock-Eye went
To tell the rest the great event.
Yet e're these hellish Saints could be
Admitted in the family,
Some regulations whereby Sinners
Might seem to win, but not be winners,

With them alike, were now drawn up,
And Sinners told to drink the cup.

And now the golden hour had come
That brought the great Millenium,
St. Carpet-Bag went on his way
Rejoicing: "All hail the day
That ushes in the great event
Whereby in wealth and long content
I pass my life! My stars for once
On me their wonted light renounce;
No more in prison must I wear
My life away and burdens bear,
At best no more in cock-loft spend
My life without a crust or friend,
With acres broad and pastures new,
A happy life will I pursue,
With but one thing requir'd to do,
To praise the Saints and share the spoil,
The Sinners damn and bless the 'loil.'"
His coadjutor, Scalawag,
Like Judas, howe'er held the bag,
But by a nice agreement made,
Both shar'd the profits of the trade,
Poor Sinners wince'd beneath the load,
While plodding on the rugged road
Of reconstruction, yet thought best
Their souls in patience were possest.
Now, throughout all Utopia
Supremely reign'd the New Idea
That all the wisdom of the past
Was only foolishness at last.
Now Christian statesmen first were found
Upon the earth—not underground,
Now was it shown beyond a doubt,
That Plato could be carried out,

Now could all heresy and schism,
All doctrine, brochure, and each ism
Be put in practice and no fool
Be standing by to ridicule.
Hail mighty era (to be plain)
Ne'er seen before, nor will again,
When all mankind stood just at par,
The Sun, the Moon, and little star,
All twinkled with an equal light
In one wide Ethiopian night,
The history past of human race
Was nothing now but common place:
No genius ever liv'd before,
No poet ever dar'd to soar
To steeps of such a giddy height
In his imaginative flight,
That could in madness thus excell
Such scenes as to this age befell.
Religious age, when law and love
Together blend and sweetly move
In unison, when politics
And piety could meet and mix,
The lion lying with the lamb,
When Truth went coquetting with Sham,
When rank conceit and impudence,
For talents pass'd and common-sense
When silly ode and sorry pun
Could vie with aught by Homer done.
When windy words in long array,
Blew great Demosthenes away;
When one wild patriotic blow
Knock'd all the props frow Cicero,
And sermons, but with folly fraught,
Surpass'd all Jesus ever taught.

A WAR BREAKS OUT IN THE HOLY CITY—GREAT CONFUSION
OCCASIONED THEREBY.

How prone are mankind when they fall,
On human nature lay it all,
And by such plea, expect to shun
A condemnation for what's done,
When Saints however fall away
From grace, as certain church-men say,
What cause on earth shall skeptics seek,
As giving clue to such a freak;
For how can sinless natures stray
In paths forbidden and away;
More so, whom, this want of power
Of self-control in such an hour
As this, when all men had agreed,
Millenium had come indeed,
Except a few poor reprobates
Like lepers standing from the gates.
But so it was, the war begun,
Altho' St. Andrew long had gone,
It seems the Saints that brought around
Millenium at length had found
Sufficient cause to break away,
From Saints whose only aim was pay,
Who under plea of holiness,
Indulging in all wickedness;
St. Carlos the alarum gave—
Expecting " a great tidal wave,"
To sweep at once from place and power
The pseudo Saints that rul'd the hour;
St. Horace, their illustrious chief,
Was figure head that lead to grief,
Behind his back a motly throng
Of noisy foll'wers, but not strong;
Fierce wax'd the fight throughout the land,
Thick fell the shafts on either hand,

The sinners were not loath to join
St. Horace, so fell into line,
St. Ulysses, who once had been
The vilest sinner ever seen,
Led on as presently we see
The loyal Saints to victory;
In sooth, the war of words that sprung,
Surpass'd all Homer ever sung,
St. Carlos launch'd out in a stream
Of calumny that shook the beam,
Of all Saintdom, so dark and deep,
That Ulysses lost all his sleep;
St. Lyman, aided by St. Carl,
Plung'd madly, in the burning marl,
The war in Heaven (pardon me),
On earth was horrible to see;
" Villain, liar, knave and cheat"
Were terms that crowded every sheet,
Whilst saintly records, (what Nemesis)
Were fairly riddled, torn in pieces;
St. Horace was as black a traitor
As e'er disgrac'd human nature,
St. Carlos base a hypocrite,
As ever liv'd and saw the light;
St. Ulysses a drunken fool,
Aspiring to monarchic rule,
St. Henry but a knave or tool,
Of his, St. Schuyler turn'd
His face to West, he had been spurned,
Kick'd out by Henry and his friends
To gratify their selfish ends;
In short, the saints of each degree,
From high to low, join'd in melee,
But Ulysses prov'd more than match,
For good St. Horace and his batch;
Them routed, horse, foot and dragoon,

Dead, dead without the hope or boon,
Of resurrection, late or soon.

GREAT CONSTERNATION IN THE NEW JERUSALEM.

It had been said by way of hint,
(So oft there seem'd be something in't,)
During this fierce and hot debate,
That something bad, or soon or late,
Would be develop'd, whereby saint
As well sinner would be taint ;
What was before a campaign lie,
And nail'd as such by sanctity,
Now took such color, shape and size
As to surpass all common lies,
So far that it was claim'd the best
To put it to the crucial test.
St. James therefore with wrathful tone,
Demanded that the facts be shown,
And order'd a committee straight
The ugly facts t'investigate.

THE EXPLOSION—THE STARS FALL FROM HEAVEN—GREAT WAILING IN THE HOLY CITY.

Had some fierce earthquake crack' the ground
And yawning abyss gap'd profound,
Surprise and fear, not have been more
Than struck each Saint upon the floor,
Who felt his deeds, when brought to light,
Would show an unmask'd hypocrite ;
They saw alas beyond recall
The hand-writing on the wall.
St. Schuyler first, oh oily Saint!
Whose smile all artists lov'd to paint,
Whose "ready, swift and tuneful tongue"
Had Virtue's charms so often sung,
The beau-ideal and model man

Built up on Christian statesman's plan,
He saw, he lied, and gave a groan,
"Othello's occupation's gone;"
Alas, all parliamentary rules
To be immur'd in Sunday Schools,
He fiercely battled to regain
His lost estate; it was in vain,
His bloody head roll'd on the floor,
And the great Smiler smiled no more;
Aye dead, and to perdition went,
For what? alas, too much per cent.
So with the rest, from day to day,
And hour to hour they pass'd away;
In life so lovely, 'twas decided,
In death they should not be divided.

THE END.

Thus ends the great experiment,
In manner needing no comment,
Save that the hardy souls who bore
The battle brunt in years before,
Came out unscathed from that fierce fire
That burnt the hypocrite and liar.
St. Carlos, now to mem'ry dear,
Thy soul was white, much as we fear
Thy head was wrong, we drop a tear
Above the dark and narrow bed,
That covers the distinguish'd dead!
St. Horace, too, no venal train
Of ideas throng'd thy busy brain,
Sleep peacefully, a nation's grief
Will follow her eccentric chief.

The ordeal past, the fever o'er,
Vex'd with Milleniums no more
That come in such a doubtful shape

And thanking God for such escape,
Mild common-sense resumes her sway,
Delirium Tremens pass'd away,
The sequel proves beyond recall,
That man is only man—that's all.

ART VS. ARTIFICE.
A DIALOGUE.

SCENE: STATUTE-ROOM, CAPITOL, WASHINGTON, D. C.

TO MY FRIEND, HORATIO STONE,

*(Who understands the circumstances under which this poem was
written, it is respectfully dedicated.)*

ARTIFICE:

Humph, sir, and then you don't believe
The end of Art is to deceive,
Nor that, unlike another trade,
It may not summon to its aid
Expedients which magnify
Yourself before the vulgar eye;
And that in no conspicuous place
True artists dare to show their face?
Nonsense! one must advertise
Their wares, or else nobody buys;
And without this, no one can rise.
I should not start to hear you say
"True Artists never work for pay,
But their reward expect to find
In unbought judgment of mankind,

Fame, or money." One can choose
Which he will take; I can't refuse
To take them both, but much prefer
A pile of lucre to the stir
My fame may make; that is to say,
I wish no fame that will not pay.

ART:

Art is Truth and Truth is Art;
Both are but parcels and a part
Of Beauty's universal law
Apelles felt and Phidias saw.
Nor can I e'er be made believe
The end of Art is to deceive;—
That it should advertise itself
By vulgar arts, producing pelf;
By tricks to catch the common eye,
Who idly gape, while standing by,
As you the facile trowel ply—
To re-adjust a shattered arm,
Purposely broke—I mean no harm—
But merely wish to criticise
What deeply pains artistic eyes.
Art has no tricks which serve to pass
Or make an artist of an ass.
Yes, I repeat all that I say—
No genuine artist dreams of pay.
E'en fame is but an afterthought
That should be neither shunned nor sought:
If given, taken as a part
Of homage mankind yields to Art,
For know you not that Genius can
Be sep'rate and distinct from man
Or woman, whom high Heaven deigns
To bear its pleasures and its pains?
That mankind worship it, yet shun

Its owner, if that such an one
Be found unworthy of that fame
That gilds a consecrated name?
Ah! know you not that artists lose
Their best existence, if they choose
The baser arts to magnify
Their ideal children, and supply
The vulgar appetite which craves
A fool befitting moral slaves;
Who, conscious of their nakedness
Of character, are wont to dress
Their basest motives in a guise
That might deceive an angel's eyes?

ARTIFICE:

Nay, not so harshly; hear me speak—
"Ends justify the means." I seek
Substantial things. You dream about
Prerequisites. I carry out
My best designs; in life 'tis art
That captivates the common heart,
And wrings from a reluctant hand
The pelf that one cannot command
By force of genius. I defy
The evil pen of calumny
To WRITE ME DOWN. It PAYS them best
To write me up; and with what zest
Their facile sentences aver,
"BLITHE ARTIFICE, none equal her."
What matter is it if I lack
True genius? I have the knack
To pacify the hungry pack
Of pseudo critics, fear no lash,
While I am well supplied with cash.
Have I not often and enough
Five dollars paid them for a puff,

And written well enough to please
A Phidias or an Apelles?
Your moral lectures will not do.
Have I in Rome not studied too?
Metaphysics are well enough
In proper places, but such stuff
Applied to Art, (I use you mild)
Is like the babbling of a child.
I find that BRUSQUENESS pays me best.
I'll take the MONEY—you the rest.

ART:

No more; I will not waste my words
On one who without blushing herds
With *parvenues*. No words reclaim
A soul that glories in its shame,
Or prostitution, if such phrase
Be apropos to one who weighs
The soul of art for what it pays.
Swindler! By Art's mighty name,
By that Brotherhood I claim,
I bid thee from my realm depart,--
Thy very presence poisons Art.
Go hence to sordid commonplace,
The rostrum mount with shameless face,
And gull the naught-denying masses
Of would-be critics, fools, and asses!
Go preach to them, and demonstrate
How soulless Art, with bitter hate,
Hath followed you, while feeling MEN
Have piped your praises with their pen.
Create around the golden calf
A sympathy in your behalf;
Teach them again, if out of mind,
"A fellow-feeling makes us kind."
Point to that weak and wanting face,

L

Of strength devoid and manly grace,
Make fools believe such is the *pose*
Of spirit mighty when the throes
Of inward conflict on it flings
A mountain of distasteful things;
Make them believe that guilty look,
That stoop of shame from life you took;
Teach them, dispite all common-sense,
You have committed no offence
'Gainst Nature first, and then to Art,
At once by this base counterpart.
Aye, teach them better, for they would
Imagine it some Robin Hood
Or Claude Duvall, with face denied
The traces of highwayman pride;
Where ev'ry look and feature pleads
But guilty to the darkest deeds.
Explain also the mighty bother
In making one leg long as "tother"—
How, had they both been parallel,
Thy *chief d'œuvre* had not stood, but fell;
To end it all, exclaim, when done,
" This is the Second Washington!"
This do, and Art may yet condone
Such grave offences to her shown:
And wounded taste a joy own
That must be foreign to her heart
While such abortions pass for Art.
Intrigue, cajole, do as you please,
But do not saddle Art with these,
Which but perpetuate disgrace
Upon the noblest of the race.
Go, and with polluted arts,
And impudence, supplanting parts
Impress the gaping crowds who gaze
With admiration at your ways;

Stand on the corners of the street,
Lift up your voice and compete
With auctioneers, and all that ilk
Who barter garden truck and milk ;
Like them enjoy that content
That springs from getting good per cent.
For bargains struck, for these are part
Of trade alone, and not of Art.
Success will follow if you try,
For there no doubt your talents lie.
There flippancy and ready wit
And want of conscience always hit.
Art has no hits ; and so, of course,
In following it, your last resource
Is wholly lost. Take my advice,
And sell thy wares, for any price
Would be a bargain to the crier—
You do not care as to the buyer.
But leave to me this hallow'd spot,
Already marr'd by many a blot.
No more. I bid the stand aside,
Since thou art WANTING found when tried.

VIRGINIA.

DEDICATED TO MY FRIEND, C. X. MATHEWS, OF WYTHEVILLE, VA.

Dear "Mac," the House adjourn'd and gone
To their constituents to condone
For past offences by a lease
On private life that shall not cease;
As was my wont when you were here,
Without affection, favor, fear,
I now resume a caustic pen

To perforate our little men.
How oft this thought comes in my head,
What boots it that a man's well read;
Why study Latin, classic Greek,
And French so well that one can speak
As fluently as *un Francais*,
When dunces rule and fools obey?
Why need one, when an eager youth
From Fiction glean as well as Truth
Such noble sentiments, to stand
Beneath the asses of the land?
He feels the pangs of keenest kind,
Who prostitutes a noble mind,
Who ever does, by tongue or pen,
For sake of pay, puff *little men*
So much that even dunces do
Believe themselves a Richelieu;
For asses have a right to bray
When genius sells itself for pay,
And rest contented with a lot,
That any blockhead might have got.
But, asses, hear me! when I vow
On you to war henceforth from now,
To wring, without remorse or dread,
The lion's skin from off your head,
Until henceforth, instead of ears,
The carcass and whole head appears:
Till he, who did for statesman pass,
Be shown just what he is—an ass.
Constituents, see the error they
Fell into on "Election Day,"
And, by experience taught and vexed,
Take care to mend it at the next.
Example apropos have we,—
A certain ass: *alias*, M. C.,
Who hither came, (let it be known,)

Whence Henry and John Randolph shone,
Who gapes and yawns, by Fortune placed,
In halls that Clay and Webster graced,
Where Randolph, with incessant wit,
Aim'd at the mark and always hit,
Where dunce and Puritanic fool
To nothing shrunk from ridicule
Heap'd on by that unsparing hand,
That flay'd the asses of the land.
And here he sits (God save the phrase)
The dunce, who would in Randolph's days,
Have been, by terms at his command,
The laughing-stock of all the land.

Virginia, great and glorious State,
Great as thou art, perforce such weight
Must sink thee, or become by rules
Infallible, the home of fools ;
Where wit and talent overslaughed,
The dunce may merit still defraud
Of all its rights, by accident
Slip into places never meant
For such as spend their lives by halves,
In breaking colts, or salting calves ;
Who without sense enough to sin
Themselves, can cry down clever men,
Whose greatest errors, as a rule,
Excel the wisdom of a fool.

Proud Mother, could'st thou substance take,
In human form for Truth's own sake,
And hither come, thine eyes would see
Thy children's pride—a mockery !
Wouldst see one son with talents fair
Enough perhaps to fill the chair
Of such societies as harp

About the merits of "Bill Arp,"
Or else explain the Golden Rule
To children of a Sunday School,
A sprightly, windy, legal chap,
Who thinks the whole world on the map,
Of his own county, which contains
Towns, mountains, rivers—but no brains;
Would'st see this son with talents fair,
Arise in place, address the Chair,
In tones that sound like squeaking hare
As urchins drag it from its lair,
While loud guffaws of laughter ring
At speaker—not the spoken thing,
Yet he, poor soul, convinc'd the while,
His wit that makes them laugh and smile,
Subsides amid a gen'ral roar,
From cloak-room, gallery, and floor,
While Mercy weeps and Justice frowns
To know thy champions are clowns!
Another, whose stentorian roar,
Like bull a neighbor's bent to gore,
Arises in his place to shake
His fist and horrid grimace make,
Tho' taxing ev'ry nerve and joint
Yet fails at last to make a point,
Subsides amid the gen'ral peal
Of merriment to make Thee feel
The stings of wounded pride and shame
At ridicule of thy proud name,
Enough to make thee curse the hour
That brought such dunces into power.

Again, behold another stands,
Look at the motion of his hands
Which chop the air as if he would
Imagine it a log of wood,

Which by incessant chops and knocks
He fain would fashion into blocks.
Out of an idea, he begun,
Now out of wind—the speech is done.

Once more, Fond Mother, strain thine eye,
See if thou can'st that vacancy!
Look, look at that imposing front,
That seat of brain where ideas hunt,
Like Noah's dove, above the deep;
Why take the dunce, he's fast asleep!

Not so, proud Mother; put up thy dagger!
Great Cæsar was no Carpet-bagger;
Stain not thy garments with the blood
"That's crept thro' scoundrels since the flood!"

Couldst thou with thine imperial eye
Behold such scenes thy heart would die
Within thee, like the virtuous dame
Of Rome, who slew herself for shame.
Great State, why should a son of thine
In thy proud annals seek to shine,
When dunce and ass and knave and fool
Not only aspire, but even rule!
Thank God, there dawns a brighter day
When talent shall resume its sway,
When accidents be made return
To breaking clods and hoeing corn,
Be taught that it is dang'rous still,
This running counter to God's will,
That all things with peculiar grace
Shine best in their appointed place;
If otherwise, expect to find
In me a stubborn foe, so kind

To all and any who desire
In their own places to aspire,
Take note, the pen jaw-bone surpasses,
For it hath slain ten thousand asses.

Miscellaneous Poems.

THE RETROSPECT.

A RAMBLING POEM, DEDICATED TO THE MEMORY OF MY MOTHER.

It is midnight now, and the silent earth
   Is wrapt in darkness, and no sound is heard
Save the lonely owl's, the halls of mirth
   Are tenantless, and, save the moaning bird,
I am alone and feeling just so near
Of being bodiless as one can be here.

The pale starlight but twinkles dimly through
   The shatter'd pane where I have bent my gaze,
Capricious sleep has bidden me adieu
   In search of those whom woe nor joy sways,
Who in bright dreams traverse the worlds of light,
And in Elysium spend the blackest night.

But why so restless, why not one resign
   His weary mind to Lethe's sweet embrace,
Or why will not our anxious hearts recline
   In Hope's sweet cradle and contrive to chase
The butterflies of fancy, as real there,
In the land of shadows, as they are elsewhere!

But none may tell why past existence
   Obtrudes itself at an unwelcome hour
And e'en conquers Nature's own resistance,
   Compelling us to retrospect and pour
The strength united of spirit soul and brain
On scenes forgotten—we cannot explain.

Yet I begin, at first, an irksome lot,
　　Recall the scenes where youthful feet first strayed ;
And, as I yield, impressions long forgot,
　　Are re-awaken'd, and the light and shade
Of former pleasures kindle in my heart
A joy, of which I dream'd not at the start.

The sweet bye-gone!　Ah, yes, the happy hours
　　Of young existence; aye the better time
Of innocent youth, ere the ripen'd powers
　　Of manhood stern connive or covet crime,
Ere passions lava, boiling in our breast,
Consumed to ashes the brightest and the best.

Till by degrees we all in sin advance,
　　Wrong in ourselves, our fellows we suspect,
A dozen outward for one inward glance,
　　That we in others may some flaw detect
To balance ours, mankind are happiest when
They are no better nor worse than other men.

There is a moral in retrospection,
　　A duty important we ever owe,
Not to ourselves, but to each connection,
　　Father, Mother, still oftener, a foe,
And if the fount of life so bitter seem
Our hands, may be, pour'd poison in the stream.

But I have wander'd, and now return
　　To sweeter thoughts of innocence and love,
To purer life, and when my soul could spurn
　　What bore no impress to the life above ;.
For though to man supplies of grace be given,
Youth is the time when he is next to Heaven.

Ah, yes! the mem'ry of some early scene,
  Made sacred and sweet by the heart's first love,
Surpasses all the sterner joys of men,
  And is just but next to a life above,
Deceitful Time may promise us far more,
But never, gives the bliss we had before.

The quaint old swing, hard by the road, where oft
  At eventide we threw all care away,
Some well-known comrade pushing us aloft,
  Then crouch'd beneath to give us greater play
For strokes more potent, that we might excel
Tom, Dick, or Harry, as the case befell.

At other times, along the shaded brook,
  "Sheeing" to comrades that they must not talk;
As in silence baiting the barbed hook,
  Or gazing intently at the dancing cork,
As luckless minnow nibbled at the bait
As if to toy with his very fate.

Ah! how our young hearts were throbbing then
  With hope and fear, and Cæsar never knew
In all his conquests such a joy as when
  Forth from the brook our shining prize we drew,
When comrades all, with wonder-waiting eyes,
Would crowd around and gaze upon the prize.

"My stars!" anon some boy would exclaim,
  "He is a whale; it is a real wonder
Your line's not broke:" soon after, vow the same,
  "Indeed the fish they just saw passing under
That ledge of rock;" while others say we struck,
What older gamblers term, "a streak of luck."

At length an urchin, smaller than the rest,
  Would, in his turn, get what he call'd "a bite;"
With mighty jerk, with force enough to wrest
  A young sea-serpent; but, oh woful sight!
The fishless hook entangled in a bough,
His mighty joy was turn'd to anguish now.

This season past, came on the dismal hour,
  When "off to school!" became the morning cry,
The boyish prayer that sudden rain might pour,
  The disappointment of a naked sky;
One joy was yet, and this, with cheer and shout,
We signalized whenever school let out.

Short-liv'd however, these idle hours
  Seem'd swifter now than when, as erst, we chased
Hope's butterflies through the pretty flowers
  That our childish fancy had so naively placed
In all lifes pathway; could such things but last
Forever, our heaven ne'er would be past.

A plain log-hut, whose walls had long withstood
  The pelting storms, until its shingles were
Far more like moss than to their native wood,
  Was first the spot where we were forc'd to hear
The name of learning; all our stock, just then,
In monosyllables—such as dog and hen.

Mountains impress us with a sense sublime;
  Hills are forgotten as we speed along,
But till the last letter of recorded time
  Has spelt our life and pronounced it wrong,
Can we forget, tho' years our sense befog,
That *dreadful* man, our primal pedagogue.

We see him still reclining in his chair,
 His legs extended and his eyes intent
Upon some problem, tugging at his hair,
 And all forgetful; we, on mischief bent,
Improv'd our chance to hurl a paper ball
At some one's head, or else against the wall.

What bashful boy does not recollect
 His first sensations as he enter'd school,
The awful stare, the quick glance to detect
 Each faulty movement, feeling like a fool,
And half resolv'd to either laugh or cry,
Without doing either, not knowing why.

The irksome hours of simulated study,
 Catching anon the ready teacher's eye,
And then an idea, undefin'd and muddy,
 Of what this means, how long to last, and why,
Until worn out he drops off in a doze,
But soon awakes, as some one pulls his nose.

Endless almost the study-hours seem
 Ere playtime comes; indeed, it is an age!
The wheel of time seems running to a team
 Of sloths and snails, while the dirty page
Of thumb-eaten primers would at once construe,
That if not learning, we are getting through.

It comes at last, but never came too soon
 For boys expectant, fond of fun and sport,
And more attractive than maps of earth or moon,
 Our playing-ground, than any map in short,
Who cares, ere he "is smit with love of learning,"
To know if earth be standing still, or turning?
 M

Let war delight the rugged hero's soul,
  Let battle fierce soothe him with bloody charms,
His ear delight the murder-telling roll
  Of musketry, and yet the clash of arms
Seems tasteless to one whom mem'ry conveys
To the mild enjoyments of his younger days.

But they have vanished: scarce enjoy'd ere gone,
  Parcel and part of all we left behind;
And scenes we knew will never more be known
  Save as a part of imperishable mind.
Like those sweet beams that gild the setting sun,
They brighten'd our youth, and their work was done.

The primer, anon, is laid aside, and then
  Came tougher studies, such as do require
A deal of thinking by heads of wiser men
  Than our good old teacher's, who could aspire
To naught beyond the "Double Rule of Three."
We pass him by—tears to his memory.

What next on programme? Boarding school of course:
  The trunk is pack'd, and off again we go,
To reap fresh sorrow from another source;
  Hard study, high price, all such things as flow
To the full complement of first-class schools,
Where all things, even food, must go by rules.

We had our share at least of rancid butter,
  Insipid hash restew'd a dozen times,—
A fluid with five full parts of water
  To one of milk,—no wonder then that rhymes
Not fit for eyes polite nor ears acute,
Adorn'd our walls, wrath cannot long be mute.

Such is the dark side, for despite all this
　There is a pleasure in the first sensation
Of being ador'd by some country Miss,
　Who deems a boarder the hope of the nation.
To be lionised is not unpleasant,
Tho' it be done by a pretty peasant.

Sweet romance! ere the youthful heart is "smit
　With the love of learning," when some fair face
Is become our idol and we worship it
　With such security that it leaves no trace
Of inward disquiet on the placid brow
For deceit and anguish are strangers now.

This is Heav'n, this the sweet Elysian
　That poets write about and lovers feel
Ere interest chills it with cold decision,
　Or age can laugh at all our mighty zeal,
Ere jealousy becomes a serious joke,
And we are hamper'd by the older folk.

But this is past, and now the little scene
　"Grows beautifully less," for cubic feet
And square root were never friends I ween
　To love and fancy; naught that may be sweet:
A sure panacea for all such ills
Is time and study, for this always kills.

And all is chang'd; too sad! for our sweetheart now
　Has ceas'd to love us, and for aught we know,
Loves a sunburnt rustic; yet she did vow
　That she did love us, and we all thought so,
But time convinc'd her we were insincere
　And she's forsaken us this many a year.

Life's battle in earnest, and all the rest
   Was but a prelude to that stern array
Of mental forces, prize to be possest,
   All that striplings crave ere ambition's day
Hath dawn'd in splender: these are but rays
That herald the comet in its lurid blaze.

Now may be seen, e'en at the midnight hour,
   The pale-fac'd student poring o'er his book,
Oblivious of all things, save the silent power
   Of his busy thoughts, as with puzzled look
He lifts his eyes and bends their steady gaze
Into night's deep darkness where the watch-dog bays.

Wrapt in fit of pleasing meditation
   He falls asleep, and fancy takes him back
To her and the little infatuation,
   That has been mention'd in his youthful track,
He sleeps an hour, and then—awakes to find
His lamp is gone, or else he must be blind.

Some little rascal, with nothing else to do,
   Performs this trick, but "look out, never mind,"
He'll "be reveng'd" and make him sadly rue
   His fine delight; for surely can he find
Some cunning *confrere* who is too willing
To give him no quarter, but a "killing."

An hour more and all the house is still
   Save the heavy snoring of the roguish chap
Who took his lamp, and on him he will
   Take his revenge as he takes his nap,
With a cat-like tread to his couch he doth go
And tieth a cord to his major toe.

Poor fellow! he is dreaming badly now;
  How his face contorts as we draw the rope,
Dreams he is falling from a summits' brow,
  And feels the last throes of expiring hope;
The pain increases and his groans begin,
Awakes, and finds that he is taken in.

These are the pleasant little interludes,
  Ere the curtain rises for another part
In the melo-drama of verbs and moods,
  A short rehearsal of the magic art,
That thrills mankind, ere from the schools we go
To garner fruit or reap the seeds we sow.

A step yet higher, and ourselves we find
  In college walls, and very soon begin
T'accommodate a grammar-sated mind
  To the rich viands of this mental inn,
Where lectures, latin and Aristotle
Are cramm'd *en masse* down our mental throttle.

Few gay professors are known to share
  The honors of professorship, but men
Whose minds were made to split a moral hair.
  And always keep their risibles within;
Whose very faces, hatchet-like and long,
Bespeak a digestion not worth a song.

Confirm'd dyspeptic, who would not pity?
  All life a blank indeed to such as he:
Without enjoyment of what is witty,
  Can drink no coffee, is forbidden tea,
Must live on food his appetite detests,
Adhere to physic, while he scoffs at jests.

It was ever thus, and as a thing of course
　　Will so remain, some blurring fault will mar:
Some hidden poison found in ev'ry source
　　Of human pleasure, clouds for ev'ry star,
And worst of all, in such a spot as this,
An old dyspeptic marr'd our college bliss.

We manag'd by some means to conciliate
　　The other professors: this wretched one
Was made for a purpose, (as if by fate)
　　To prove experience does not faulty run:
That Nature ne'er forsakes a gen'ral rule,
To pacify impetuous boys at school.

Perennial joy has never yet been found,
　　Tho' sought by all in this world of sorrow;
Some discord dwells e'en in the sweetest sound;
　　Man without trouble will contrive to borrow;
One little ill he nurses, till a score
Fill up the void, where was but one before.

Some men are vile, immeasurably vile,
　　Grac'd with an angel, (pardon us, a wife,)
Are never cheerful in her loving smile:
　　Their preference seeming on the side of strife,
Which seems more congenial to their natures
Than all the grace of angelic creatures.

Poor wife! in one moment she cannot tell
　　What follows next: "Did I not tell you so;
The meat is overdone, the bread is stale,
　　Pray tell me Madame, I should like to know;
And the tea and coffee, God help the cook,
Or the wife, whose business was to overlook!"

No accident on either field or farm
    But what she gets an undeserving share
Of cutting speeches; innocent of harm
    And ready to obey, yet he does not spare :
And still such men seem to have better wives
Than good men get, who spend such wretched lives.

Reader, this is no connected story
    As you can see; our former theme
Was the old professor, whose greatest glory
    Tormenting youth, we now recur to him :
And at this point, before we deviate,
Occurr'd an episode, which we relate.

Hard by the college walls there us'd to feed
    A steady farmer, all his flocks and herd ;
Among the rest a weather-beaten steed,
    "Old as the hills," this fact has been averred
By at least a dozen, who seem'd to know
How old the hills were: this no matter though.

One stormy night six of us sallied forth
    With ropes and bridle to secure the prize,
His foretop seiz'd; the bridle in his mouth,
    And led him back, no bandage to his eyes,
For he was blind, and should he get away,
Be catechised, he could but answer, "nay."

The old professor had a lecture-room
    Reach'd by a stair, and hereat we proposed
To play our joke, and if not all, get some
    Revenge for wrongs we suffer'd and supposed,
So to this room with muffled feet we bore
Bucephalous, came out and shut the door.

As to our programme, it was merely this:
   To put our prize in the professor's room,
And lest our meaning should seem amiss,
   Adorn him with goggles and thus assume
To be professor, or some other fraud,
Whom genteel people have long since outlawed.

So in this hall, where so much wisdom sat,
   The poor old steed went idly tramping round;
Long, lank and lean, and blind as any bat,
   Unconscious, too, for aught we knew, of sound:
Back to our beds with stealthy steps we trod,
Await events to come with morning's god.

The morning came, and yet no one could tell.
   How came this creature to a hall of learning,
Some boy guess'd; no boy guesses well
   At such a time, his talent for discerning
Effects and causes is confus'd and weak,
And his true opinion submits to " check."

" Thanks," we had no little George and hatchet
   Within our ranks, and yet we could not lie;
Had been in scrapes, and knew how to match it,
   Which was, when question'd, to utter no reply;
The college court in solemn conclave met
To sift the case and see what they could get.

Now, old dyspeptic had before foresworn
   His solemn purpose to at once depart
Unless the offender were made to mourn
   In penance first and feel the bitter smart
Of quick expulsion, for he would not stay
Where disrespect were shown him night and day.

It must be fated that all bands of men,
  Howe'er cordial and compact they be,
Must nourish some traitor, or spy within,
  Exposing secrets better men than he,
But perhaps no wiser, have to him imparted,
Base, treach'rous and false and hollow-hearted.

Ours was exception to the gen'ral rule,
  All our comrades faithful to the letter,
The grim professor bade adieu to school,
  He vengeance vowing—we felt the better:
Supreme contempt and united action
Had prov'n superior to the college faction.

Hours of emulation, when prose essays
  In Greek and Latin the order of the day,
The cramming art, a hundred other ways
  Mankind invent for making a display
On set occasions, when multitudes repair
To places nam'd, to be astonish'd there.

The day is come, to us the dreadful day,
  Known as "commencement," and the building rings
With rival bands, and when professors gray
  In learning's service, and other bookish things
Are in abundance in conspicuous places,
With multitudes peering into their pale faces.

Our sweethearts too are in attendance then
  To torture us with their expectant eyes,
Which more than say, "Now quit yourselves like men,
  And don't forget to win my promis'd prize!"
The prize is won and our bliss complete,
And our loved one's glances make it doubly sweet.

The farce is ended, and gladly we receive
   Well-earn'd diplomas, and at once depart
To other fields, where merit can achieve
   Its sure reward, and where no pert upstart
Can rob us of them, and where our deeds decide
Whether the judges were deceiv'd, or lied.

II.

Sweet Mother, much mine erring feet have strayed
   In paths forbidden alike by God and man!
Tho' I have drain'd sin's veriest dregs and made
   My life a curse and marr'd the heav'nly plan
Of my redemption, never at thy door
Can this be laid, I am alone impure.

The senseless clods inclose the narrow urn
   That contains thy ashes; this heart of mine
Shall inclose thy mem'ry while life shall burn,
   And a ceaseless fire at its altars shine
In silent worship at the shrine of one
Who was my Mother; but I now have none.

Ah, Mother, if ever in thy pure abode
   Of bliss celestial, a prayer be made
For tempted mortals, groaning 'neath a load
   Of leaden sorrow in a land of shade,
Pray thou for one whose early misspent
Would of his sins in riper years repent!

For next to God and his Anointed Son,
   A Mother knows the nature of her child,
Its very soul and hers are partly one,
   Since from its birth an heir to passions wild;
She nurses it from infancy to man,
In that short life, which is at best a span.

Standing above thy dark and narrow bed,
   And looking at it, comes the solemn thought,
I may have wrong'd or griev'd the hallow'd dead,
   Gave harsh replies when I should have said naught,
By evil deeds inflicted wo and pain,
In secret caus'd her tears to flow like rain.

No more of this; such thoughts would break my heart,
   Grieve Thee in Heav'n had they but access there.
From life's dark side and to the brighter part
   I gladly turn and seek again to share
In thy remembrance—that of joys past,
When Thou wert with me, and time sped fast.

Oh, merry youth! I love to dwell with thee:
   A thread of romance permeating all
The magic cord that thrills and raptures me
   Whene'er touch'd, or, when I it recall,
A bright existence stretching to the fount
Of life almost, I take into account.

Romantic hours! ere solid science came
   To strip us of phantasies, and when the sound
Of growling thunder and the lurid flame
   Of zigzag lightnings were strangely bound
With deeper mysteries, unseen by eyes,
Whose end of faith is what they scrutinize.

I see again the aged cherry tree
   With all its sweet and luscious fruit, where I
At eventide, from school restrictions free,
   Have nimbly climb'd and threw down from on high
Some pretty bunch, and hop'd thereby to gain
A smile from Lucy or a kiss from Jane.

A first love: can there, will there, ever be
   A mem'ry to come so heav'nly as this;
So gilded with sanctity, and so free
   From dregs that spoil the cups of riper bliss?
Will e'er rainbow as sweet again arise
To gladden our hearts or thus adorn our skies?

And then the days of feasting, "dining day"
   As it was call'd, when Dick and Harry came
To sport with me; meanwhile our parents stay
   About the house, discussing duck and game,
While we, not cumber'd with such weighty themes,
Rov'd thro' the fields, or paddled in the streams.

Ah, me; since nevermore shall I with joy
   See them again, the senseless, silent earth
Contains the form of many a charming boy,
   My boon companions, gone from scenes of mirth
To endless life; by far a sweet exchange
Of earthly bliss for Heaven's boundless range.

One fair-hair'd brother went early to his grave,
   Bedew'd with tears that mothers only shed
O'er the bier of a lov'd one, ere she gave
   The hallow'd kiss, and then the narrow bed
Receiv'd the body yielded to its trust,
Till God again shall raise it from the dust.

Others surviv'd and bore with me the brunt
   Of deadly battle, when the leaden hail
Mow'd down the gallant hearts that stood in front,
   And the death-angel call'd them to its pale,
Their bones lie bleaching on battle-field and plain,
Their bodies only—their souls were ne'er slain.

Now far remov'd from each familiar scene
    Of early life, I'm fated to survey
The sea of blood that rolls its depths between
    All that I loved, ere came the direful day
When sounds of conflict rent the Southern sky,
And "Dixie's Land" became the battle-cry.

Our land was girt within, without with foes,
    And we were toss'd as when a leaf is torn
From its parent stem by a gale that blows
    From chance's realm and is then idly born
Where'er it lists : four years of blood and strife,
Ere we could lick our batter'd limbs to life.

Corruption follows carnivals of blood,
    Impregns the State with its pernicious seeds,
Breaks down the teachings of the great and good,
    Depletes the Treasury while the nation bleeds
At ev'ry pore and then evades the same
By easy pardons, and glories in the shame.

But these are days of shame : men glory now
    In deeds a heathen would not dare to do ;
Black infamy would rest upon their brow,
    And that in lands whose gods are not the true.
Why prate of Progress ?   Until we cleanse
Our Augean stables, fear not foreign sins.

Look in those Halls where Clay and Webster shone,
    Where Calhoun, dignified, severe and grave,
Respect commanded, where Benton's tone
    Rang out to all and full assurance gave
Of innate greatness ; see a people's pride
The laughing-stock for all the world beside !
    N

Dumb-founded ignorance in those sacred chairs,
   And corruption stalking in all its shapes
Hating that greatness, which at best but shares
   The sympathies of few! How can such apes,
Who dwell on honesty, a thing they never knew,
Attempt reforms?—their downfall if they do.

Immortal Plato! never yet hath man
   Approach'd thine ideal; ruin and decay
Sap all the pillars of thy perfect plan;
   Corruption sweeps the edifice away.
Great Rome it took three centuries to die,
But ours totters ere a decade goes by!

What boots it now if that a despot's sway
   Or sceptred monarch be our Fed'ral head?
Thy spirit, Freedom, long since pass'd away!
   We court thy shadow and worship in thy stead
A hollow mockery; our love is lust!
Our liberty, license! false gods our trust!

From scenes so sick'ning in disgust we turn
   Our mind's eye backward, ling'ring to survey
The purer life for which our spirits yearn,
   The rosy hours of boyhood's brighter day,
And strive with sweet illusions to forget
Our country's shame, our sun of glory set.

'Tis not our wish nor purpose to imbrue
   Our souls in seething pools, but cultivate
A love for beauty from a lofty view,
   O'erlooking (if can be) our ruin'd State;
Convinc'd, at last, some hero will arise,
Avenge our wrongs—give freedom to our skies.

IMOGEN.

When she is seen,
Mine eyes behold
A being cast
In Beauty's mould,
Whose presence more
Than breathing clay,
Or soulless things
That pass away;
Her eyes have more
Than brilliant glance;
They have the charm
Of sweet romance;
Her lips speak more
Than utter'd words,
Or dulcet notes
Of soulless birds;
Her life is more
Than merely human;
Her being more
Than merely woman;
A child of light
Beneath the skies,
An angel in
An earthly guise;
She's Heav'n's best,
Vouchsav'd to man,
The keystone in
Creation's plan;
The fairest gift,
The brightest gem
That decks creation's
Diadem.

Sweet Lady! born
To beautify
With sweetest charm
The social sky!
Who looks on thee
Except to love,
Is dead to all
The joys above.
The dull in soul
Mayhap can see
No real charm;
Not so is he,
Whose soul hath kept,
In spite of fate,
Some tokens of
Its first estate.
Sweet Maid of dark
Celestial eyes,
May Heaven's sweet,
Serenest skies
Look down on Thee,
Where'er Thou art!
So sweet in mind,
So pure in heart.

SOME TRUTHS ABOUT LYING.

If lying be "the vice of slaves,"
And cheating added, that of knaves,
Then cheating, lying, both combined,
Are parts and parcels of mankind.
The maiden lies to save her beaun
From what old bell-dames wish to know;
The merchant lies to make a cent,

Says "what he says, is what he meant;"
The fashionable ladies say,
"Pray, won't you call another day!
I am so pleas'd to see;" oh, no,
She meant so pleas'd to see you go;
The luckless suitor raps the door,
His sweetheart, on the upper floor,
Tells Agnes, when this beau shall come,
To say, "Young Miss is not at home."
Perhaps she meant this lie to trim,
By meaning not at home—for *him.*
But then, some old philosopher,
Whose name we need not mention here,
Has given the philosophy
Of what is properly a lie;
And lying, if we may believe
His theory, is to deceive:
If so, there's not a grain of doubt,
We were all liars, if found out.
Who ever "wishes pleasant day"
To bores, who wear his life away,
Is lying; and he knows it too,
And damns him ere he's out of view.
Who has not felt a sense of pain
When saying "Wont you call again?"
Nor felt as if his gizzard smiled,
When forc'd to praise an ugly child?
What is the reason, then, we ask?
Truth's too severe, and needs a mask.
It would not do to say on sight,
"Why, Miss, you are a perfect fright,"
Nor damn the coffee, when it takes,
The skin from off your tongue and makes,
The tears come welling in your eye,
Nor seem'd perplex'd when babies cry;
When toes are crush'd you must not wince,

But say politely, "no offence!"
When Miss is homely you must pay
Your compliments, or she will say,
In secret to another lass,
"There sits a most provoking ass!
I wonder why the fates invent
Men so devoid of sentiment!
To say the least, he might have said
A good word for the book I read,
And complimented me, instead
Of beauty, on my classic head.
The book so full of life and flash,
The brute pronounc'd 'all silly trash;'
Instead of this, occasion took
To compliment a stale old book
Which treats about the 'moral law'
Of which I never read or saw."
Do parsons lie? Yes, even they
Are piously inclin'd that way
When not too strict in what they say,
And frequently, to make a point,
Knock truth and reason out of joint.
Do politicians too? Oh, my!
To ask if politicians lie!
Reader, what are we to do;
What line in life shall we persue
If this philosophy be true?
The best we can—which means, no doubt,
Be careful what we talk about.

MY IDEAL.

Sweet Lady, I confess thou art
The charming idol of my heart,
The beau-ideal of my mind,
The highest type that it could find
Of beauty, wit, and soul combined.
God gave thee, with a lavish hand,
A mind that could all clay command,
An eye that beams with such a ray
As thine, I will not meet for aye,
A mouth that speaks for one so young,
What would become an older tongue ;
That nice, discriminating grace,
That even now abstractions trace,
Assigning them their proper place,
That truthful, analytic skill,
That tells a mountain from a hill,
And wit,—withal the best of it,
'Tis not a man's,—but woman's wit ;
No meteor's flash, whose light consigns
To darkness those for whom it shines ;
No sudden and sarcastic cut ;
No daubing decency with smut ;
No agile antics on the line,
'Twixt what is gross and what is fine ;
No sentence with a double sense,
That leaves an audience on the fence ;
No member of that petty clan,
Who must be witty when they can,—
Not when they should,—and therefore strike
At foes and bosom friends alike,
Who, fearing that a chance be lost,
Will use their tongue at any cost :

Thy wit is classified and found
With those who please, not those who wound.
The brilliant lightning of thy mind
Will strike, nor wish to slay mankind;
And by the lamp's unsteady light
I think of thee, bright one, to-night,
Can see the eye, where genius burns,
And love and sympathy by turns,
Can see the proud imperial air
That only queenly natures wear;
The whole bright, intellectual face
Is beaming on me as I trace
Thy picture on the written scroll,—
Queen of my heart, and mind, and soul!
Can hear thy wit's incessant flash
In ridicule of cant and trash,
Can see the pretty lips that move
My mind to act—my heart to love;
Unlike all others I have known,
Unique, original, alone;
A noble woman who can sway
The soul of man in beauty's way,
Who charms him in his saddest hours
By converse and her winning powers,
Whose graces and whose smile of light
Might charm a gloomy anchorite
And cause him to regret the spell,
That binds him to his lonely cell,
A feeling, sentimental mind,
A heart benevolent and kind,
An ideal one, and all possest
With charms and gifts to make us blest,
Who, 'mid the cares of busy life,
Can beauty see apart from strife.
Where darkness blinds the vulgar way,
She sees the beams of golden day

With mental eye, but form'd to pierce
The beauties of the Universe,
A mind of far too fine a mould
A common ideal to behold,
And yet imbued with ev'ry power
That could beguile misfortune's hour,
A sympathetic, feeling heart,
A mind discerning truth from art.
Queen of the realm my Fancy made
Ere I had known her, who has swayed
My heart like some one from above,
Impelling, not imploring, love;
For these and many reasons more,
Thou art the ——, (pardon,) I adore,
The matchless grace of one so young,
With such a mind so finely strung.

THE REFUGE.

Into regions ideal
I fly from the real
With delight, just so oft as I can;
  From the " bricks and the straw,"
  From the curse of the law
Blind matter has impos'd upon man.

From the horrible spell,
From the shadows of Hell,
I soar to my own native Heaven,
  And I bask in the light
  And the freedom from night
That God to my spirit hath given;

And my soul it forgets
All its pangs and regrets,
The perfect is a stranger to pain ;
And the music I hear
Is so faultless and clear
That an Angel must utter the strain !

And the place is replete
With all that is sweet,
In all shapes that existence can give.
Oh, Heaven ; that I might
Ever dwell in thy light,
Aye ever in the ideal to live !

I am sure that no clog
Would my senses befog
Or drag me again to the real ;
But assur'd of the truth
Of perennial youth,
Age never can dim the ideal.

TO A LITTLE LADY.

Of size diminutive, and yet
'Tis thus, for Nature could not get,
In all her countless stores complete,
Material more for one so sweet ;
In truth, she had no dust to spare
In making one so sweet and rare.
Her eyes, to show the finest thought,
Are matter to perfection wrought,
And yet expressing none the less
A world of sprightly roguishness,
Whose glimpses in a moment show

All artists dream or poets know,
The spirit-windows in whose glance
Are worlds of beauty and romance,
A brow on which artistic eyes
Could dwell forever, nor comprise
Their beauty true, as well to try
To paint the lightning of the sky,
The lilly or the blushing rose
Or beauty, which *arc-en-ciel* throws
Athwart the eastern sky at even,
When clouds obscure that part of Heaven,
A hand, whose very prettiness,
Makes every touch seem a caress,
While mouth and chin, and lips and nose,
Accord, and *en rapport* with those.

No bird that deftly wings the air,
With carol sweet or plumage fair,
But 'minds me of the joy that springs
From her, as if my soul took wings
At her command, to soar above
All other thoughts except to love,
Her charms are such as win their way
Despite what reason has to say,
Hers is the magic power that wrings
A sweetness from the dullest things,
That gives to life, by more than half,
The sweetest nectar that we quaff.
The weather, latest styles of dress,
Or aught her lovely lips express,
To me, by far, are sweeter things
To listen to than talk of Kings,
A voice whose bewitching tone
An angel might be proud to own
And doubtless is, all other things
Of theirs is hers, except their wings,

A being bright as Fancy's beam,
The real of a lovely dream,
A soul that sanctifies its clay,
A picture that must dwell for aye
In every eye allow'd to trace
But once the features of her face,
A mind so exquisitely made,
Portraying every light and shade
Of thought, and feeling, one may trace
Their lights and shadows in her face;
No more, save all perfection given,
Is hers, allowed one under Heaven.

A REMINISCENCE.

Last eve, as on my couch I lay,
My spirit wander'd far away
Into the past, and did recall
My youth, my early life and all,
Until I felt the bursting joy
That thrill'd my bosom when a boy,
When brook and field, and fruit and sky
Lent Heaven to my youthful eye.
Ah, days of youthful innocence,
Ere pleasure pall'd upon my sense,
When sitting on a Mother's knee
She sang some simple song for me,
Told me the story of the Cross,
Of Adam's fall and Eden's loss,
Then of the brighter world above,
Where all was happiness and love;
At other times my Father told
Of heroes in the days of old,

The while my wonder-waiting eyes
Evincing joy and surprise.
Thus was my young mind early taught
To dwell upon the noblest thought
That even mov'd me when a boy
My time, my talents to employ,
If I should live to man's estate,
Do something either good or great.
When manhood came, I walk'd in pride
With one that lov'd me at my side,
Her face was fair; I did not know
How soon the dream would change to woe;
I did not deem the heart she gave
So worthless, yet I was her slave,
Obedient to each beck and nod,
And lov'd her better than my God!
But proven false, I threw aside
The bands in scorn and sullen pride,
Resolved at once I would be free
And live for those who live for me,
Became ambitious, dar'd to soar
To heights I had not dream'd before,
Built heavens of my own, wherein
No traces of deceit or sin,
Plung'd deep in speculative lore
Concerning things not known before
By me, until my brain would reel
With thoughts I could not name but feel.
I left my boyhood's home and went
To strangers, aye in banishment;
An exile, leaving far behind
All that had pleas'd or pain'd my mind.
Long years had pass'd in rapid pace
Ere I had seen a Sister's face,
When back to scenes of youth I came
Among my kindred and my name.

O

SPECULATION.

Tho' deeply metaphysics teach
   The freedom of the will,
And fondly theologians preach
   Its powers and its skill;

Yet who may know the secret springs
   That prompt each word or deed,
What gives to thought its airy wings
   That distance lightning's speed?

Or why this mighty impulse given
   To deeds of sin and death,
Unless it be propulsion-driven,
   Inherited from breath?

Then if such forces should impel,
   Nor leave the spirit free,
Why hath each heart its secret hell
   For deeds that can but be?

And conscience, too, is this a name
   Unknown, yet us'd by all?
Were education all the same,
   Who then could tell its thrall?

The savage breast is made to feel
   Its pangs in other ways
Than ours; perhaps mistaken zeal,
   Which prejudice conveys.

In speculation we are lost
   Beyond the written Word;
The seas of doubt cannot be cross'd
   When God will not be heard!

But men all make their future beds,
    For better, or for worse;
Yet fain would pile on other heads
    The mountain of their curse.

THE DRUNKARD'S LAMENT.

"I mourn the hours wasted
    In revelry and wine,
And o'er the bitter memories
    That now around me twine,
Of hopes and ruin'd fortunes
    I've squander'd long ago,

Of friends who have forsaken
    Me in the days of wo!
Alas, where are the faces
    That us'd to greet me then?
And where the boon companions
    Who led me on to sin?

Some lie in graves dishonored;
    A few are living yet,
The bright star of whose being,
    Like mine, forever set;
The tumult of carousals,
    The lewd and leering stare,

Are present with me ever,
    Like spectres of despair!
The blood of noble spirits
    Is now upon my head,
For many youths of promise
    I into ruin led!

My good and praying Mother
Long sank beneath the blow!
These—bitter recollections:
Would God they were not so!
My gentle Wife, that lov'd me,
Alas! where is she now?

Her ashes are reposing
Where weeping willows bow!
My base and cruel treatment
Soon drove her to despair;
Her tender heart was broken
By grief it could not bear!

My pretty, cherub children
Are sleeping at her side,
For there was none to nurse them
When their sweet Mother died!
In age, alas! forsaken
By God, as well as man;

No human soul can love me,--
Inhuman if it can!
Oh, soul-destroying poison,
I'm wholly now thy slave
And have no other hope than—
To fill a drunkard's grave!

AMBITION.

INSCRIBED TO MY YOUNG FRIEND, M. T. M****.

Strike out, oh! free-born soul, strike out!
  Who are the imperial few,
But mighty ones, who dar'd to doubt
  Existing systems when untrue!

Let birds of timid wing alone
　　In circles small their flight confine,—
"All man has done may still be done,"
　　Be hence thy watchword and thy sign.

Behold the long array of names,
　　Whose deeds, thro' ages, cannot die:
Their thoughts still breathe like tongues of flame—
　　This, this is immortality!

"Dare disbelieve till proof is shown,"
　　Save where the Finite yields to God;
Examine all things, cling to none,
　　Be more than merely breathing clod;

Let commonplace delight the dull,
　　Seek thou the noble and the great—
Earth never was, nor will be full
　　Of heroes; honors still await.

Oh Fame! next word to God alone—
　　Let feeble intellects decry—
For next to the Almighty One
　　I worship thee, for thee I sigh.

Who covets dark oblivion's bed
　　Is dead in soul and cannot see,
On high delights has never fed;
　　In common with the beasts is he.

Thy mind is made of finer mould,
　　With less affinity for clay,
Than his who merely worships gold,
　　Or things that perish in a day.

Heed not the taunts of jeering fools,
　　Let them contented live and die,
The pliant necks and willing tools,
　　Whose praise a penny still can buy.

Seek Thou some sunny isle of Truth,
　　Unknown as yet in Error's main,
And consecrate thy mind, thy youth,
　　To seek it thro' a life of pain.

Thou hast a mind that dares to stray
　　From dusty highways ever trod
By sweating millions ere your day,—
　　And highways seldom lead to God.

Let all things nerve your soul to try
　　Heights inaccessible as yet ;
With Hope thy Mother's heart beats high,
　　Be thou her Pride and not her Pet.

Thought never yet enslav'd a mind—
　　Think deeply if Thou wouldst be free ;
Few were the slaves of human kind,
　　Could Thought but teach them how to see.

Aim high ; the aim directs the shot,—
　　Ambition is the gift of God,—
Explore the hidden realms of thought,—
　　Thou art a spirit, not a clod ;

Once right, put all thy fears to rout,
　　Break thro' the dull array of rules,
Waste not thy heaven-sent powers about
　　Concerns which only trouble fools ;

Think boldly, act upon the spot,
  In God alone of Battles trust,
Let souls in dull oblivion rot,
  Like worms, which only love the dust.

Dear Montague, I hope to trace
  The paths of glory blest, with Thee;
To run an intellectual race
  Whose goal is immortality.

Tho' diverse paths our souls may take—
  Mine seeks the hidden heights of song—
But let thine dare, and it shall shake
  The spheres of villainy and wrong.

When the relentless plow of Time
  Has furrow'd both our cheek and brain,
May then, as now, the "true Sublime"
  Be ours to seek,—'tis ours to gain.

Aye, make the world in which you live
  The better for thy dwelling here,
Thy hand, thy tongue, thy talents give
  For what is noble without fear.

Then shall the nations, in their love,
  To thee deserving tribute pay,
Tho' dead, thy name shall live above
  The fameless millions of to-day.

WHEN HOPE IS EXTINGUISHED.

When hope is extinguish'd and joy is fled,
  And the flowers of love lie withered and dead,
They do not remove, but all lie entombed,
  In the grave-yard of memory in which they once bloomed.

They breathe no perfume as they did in the past,
  Of beauty bereft by adversity's blast;
No more shall we see their sweet petals again,—
  The trunk of their mem'ry alone shall remain.

All the rainbows of hope, which painted the sky,
  Did vanish when it saw love's flowers all die,
The abode of sweet hope was chang'd into woe,
  When banished and died all the flowers and *bow.*

WHY I AM SAD.

'Tis not some dark and secret sin,
  That cause the woes which lurk within,
Nor conscience smiting in my breast,
  For sins too foul to be confessed.

The mounful secret I will tell:
  I lov'd not wisely, but too well,
I did not deem that woman's art,
  Was trifling with a trusting heart.

Nor did I deem a face so fair,
  Should ever drive me to despair,
Nor 'till that hour did I know
  Love was another name for woe.

Too soon, alas! my youthful heart
　Was deeply pierced by sorrow's dart,
Its brightest hopes too soon destroyed
　For time to quickly fill the void.

When clouds my brow shall overcast,
　Look not on me, but on the past,
Where Hope has liv'd, and sunk, and died,
　And left me naught but sullen pride.

THE DRUNKARD'S SEPARATION.

" In the cold and dreary winter,
　When the birds had ceas'd to call,
　When Mother Earth was mantled
　As with a funeral pall;
　In the cold and bleak December
　When the flowers all had faded
　And o'er the face of Nature
　A silence deep pervaded,
　It was then I stood before one
　Whose love had been my all,
　And heard in mournful accents
　These tones of sorrow fall:
　' The past, with all its pleasures,
　I bid thee now forget;
　I sigh with bitter sorrow
　That we have ever met.
　Each token of endearment,
　Each look and loving mien
　Give way, and only coldness
　Appear where love hath been;
　The chain of love that bound us,
　Alas! is sever'd now!

But this had never happened
Hadst thou only kept thy vow.
Ah, had you lov'd so fondly
Me, as the deadly bowl,
The curse of sweeter hours
Had never marr'd thy soul!
Say not I do not love Thee;
The past too well can prove
How fond was my devotion,
How earnest was my love!
But I will never follow
The drunkard in his path;
Beneath are stinging serpents,
Above, eternal wrath!'

'Tis hard, when hope is blighted,
To check the rising sigh,
Or stop the burning teardrop
That sparkles in the eye;
'Tis hard to feign a coldness,
Indifference at best,
When the heart's intensest passions
Are striving in the breast;
'Tis hard to quench the fire
In hearts, and not of earth;
'Tis hard to crush the flowers
Of a celestial birth!"

SUBMISSION.

My soul, in calm defiance now,
　At length hath settled down;
I care not tho' the world may smile,
　Nor do I dread its frown.

It seems at times as tho' my heart
　Were wholly made of steel,
At other times incarnate fiends
　Might pity what I feel.

Thro' all the trial-harden'd soul,
　Tho' wrung with anguish now,
Which sorrow like a tempest shakes,
　Yet will not deign to bow.

Beat then, ye cruel storms of woe,
　On a devoted head
Ye cannot quell the stubborn heart
　Which lives, tho' hope is dead.

A hope of earth and not of Heaven,—
　Not that delusive snare,—
For tho' all earthly hope hath fled,
　Mine are immortal there.

But once my heart lov'd earthly toys,
　With all its strength and power,
But wisely shuns the poison now
　That lurks in ev'ry flower.

'Tis best that ev'ry hope should die,
　For which I once have striven,
Yet leave me that immortal one—
　The blessed hope of Heaven.

ON LEAVING VIRGINIA.

Farewell, ye hills and mountains blue,
Which long have charm'd my youthful view!
Farewell each dear remember'd spot,
I leave you all, but ne'er forgot!
Soon, soon, must miles between us lie
And other scenes salute mine eye;
But while I seek another shore,
And leaving all I lov'd before,
My heart will ever fondly turn
To Old Virginia and yearn,
For every friend I left behind
Will dwell forever in my mind.

THE FIRST KISS.

Love's magical fingers touch'd the chords of my song,
  Tho' feeble, an echo which has slumber'd too long.
Neither music nor nature, my spirit could move,
  Till its voice was waken'd by the first kiss of love.

Tho' Judas his Master did betray with a kiss,—
  Still no one supposes that a pretty young Miss,
While a lover implants this test of affection,
  Would banish its joy with the sad recollection?

When two young hearts are beating in unison sweet,
  Who would deem for a moment their bliss was complete,
Till by mutual concurrence its power they prove,
  And banish all their doubts in the first kiss of love?

TWILIGHT.

'Tis sweet, when daily toil is ended,
  To seek out some sequester'd shade,
Where light and darkness, gently blended,
  Are emblems of the life we lead.

Beholding, at this tranquil hour,
  The heavens' starry dome of night,
All earthly objects lose their power
  To check the spirits upward flight.

As onward thro' the viewless air,
  Ascending to the realms of bliss,
It sees all forms of beauty there,
  For which it vainly sought in this.

The planets and revolving spheres
  Are pass'd, and on the spirit flies
Beyond the realms which reason fears:
  The nameless islands of the skies.

The limits of permitted thought,
  The line which God has thrown between
Himself and man : we reach, we halt,
  Where depths divine all supervene.

Returning, scarce we wish to gaze
  At all on sublunary things,
But dull inertia soon repays
  The bliss we feel upon our wings.

Low appetites and lofty will
  Resume their wonted war again,
The spark that oceans cannot kill
  Soon yields to gentle Morpheus' reign.
      P

WHEN LOOKING ON THEE, LUCILE.

When looking on thee, Lucile,
  On beauty's form and essence,
I drink nectarian sweetness,—
  The poetry of thy presence.

Thy dark eyes fitful flashes,
  Whose light cannot be given
From any other sources,
  Than such as spring in Heaven.

All that is sinless, stainless,
  That a human heart may know,
I feel when I am with Thee,
  Beauty ever made me so.

Lucile, thy name awaketh
  Sweetest raptures in my breast,
Like that which music maketh
  When so tenderly expressed.

A concord of sweet music,
  It falleth upon my ear,
Like music o'er waters floating
  When the air is still and clear.

THE METHODISTS.

'Tis true you are a whining crew,
And fond of some excitement,
Nor wholly guiltless can you plead,
In thought, or action, word, or deed,
To scriptural indictment.

But there are others, call'd your brothers,
Of a rather colder breed,
Who seem to think, altho' they wink,
You have not the proper creed.

Methinks I see a little crowd,
Who leave the strife of tumult loud,
And get beneath the shade,
And strive out there to split a hair
Of metaphysics here and there,
While mercy calls for aid.

The Devil gathers up the sheaves,
And, altho' laughing in his sleeves,
Keeps feigning melancholy;
Because anon a prayer is read,
Think they the Devil can be dead—
What blindness and what folly!
If all the earth but knew the worth
Of one immortal soul,
We'd have less cant how Wesleyan's rant,
And far more feelings to control.

TO A DECEIVER.

Smile on, fair one, thou may'st deceive
    The heart of some unwary youth,
And cause some stripling to believe
    Thy vows and pledges are but truth.

Some heedless youth who may not know
    The wiles of a deceiver's heart,
Nor see the fiend which lurks below
    The face that acts an angel's part.

TEARS.

Of what avail are all our tears,
  And sighs that almost rend the heart,
When not one pleasing prospect cheers,
  But has its own dark counterpart?

Yet impulse has a thousand eyes,
  Where boasting reason has but one,
And not a thing survives, or dies,
  That reason loves to dwell upon.

Youth, innocence, and hoary age,
  Are phases in the life of all;
The bard, philosopher, and sage,
  Alike in common ruin fall.

And tears and sighs alike are found
  In each successive stage we live,
Each moment has a dart to wound,—
  We must receive as well as give.

But man is strongest when he weeps,
  Light as a stoic deems a tear,
The proof convincing that he keeps
  Some better feelings—even here.

Lives there a man surviving all
  Life's changes with a stolid ease,
That man has fallen 'neath the fall:
  A being devils love to please.

Our very weakness is our might;
  When reason halts, faith leads the way,
And reason leads the mind in night;
  Faith ushers in the golden day.

But tears; yes, sacred, holy tears,
  Our great Creator deign'd to shed,
His nature infinite appears
  As much in this as all he said.

What then, if tears a traitor prove
  We all must trust until betrayed,
Worse is the man no tears can move
  Than beasts: them pity can invade.

To me, above the hopes of fame
  Are they still dearer, as I trust
My memory a tear will claim
  When I am silent in the dust.

ADIEU ROMANCE.

Adieu, Romance, adieu!
  'Tis time that we should part,
For there's no balm in you
  To soothe a blighted heart.

Realities, thy vassals,
  Have soar'd above thee high
Since all thy gilded castles
  In ghastly ruin lie.

Where are thy realms of pleasure?
  Where now thy seats of bliss,
That were my chiefest treasure
  In such a world as this?

A VISION.

Alone in an attic, a poet sat musing
  And dreaming of joys then vanish'd or past,
Sighing still for the pleasures that perish in using:
  Flowers that wither from adversity's blast.

His face wore an aspect of sorrow and sadness,
  As tho' disappointment had darken'd his youth
And robb'd ev'ry feature of traces of gladness,
  By a stern, altho' necessitous truth.

Yet his was a sorrow so still and so solemn
  That language essay'd not to breathe it;
Like a mourner's, who gazes at the death-telling column,
  As he thinks of the lov'd one beneath it.

But at once a vision of sadness came o'er him
  Subdued as the sound of whispering air;
The ghost of past pleasure that flitted before him,
  And fill'd his dark mind with a sense of dispair.

" Young Dreamer," it mutter'd, " whence cometh the sadness
  That now o'ershadows and darkens thy heart ?
Dismiss these creations—the genius of madness,
  Which trouble thy mind with a sorcerer's art!

Oh, seize the bright present and forsake the dark past.
  Nor grope in its ruins, hoping to find
A flower unwither'd by adversity's blast,
  Its ashes create no more of its kind!"

This friendly monition once given, it vanished—
  Silently, softly, as when it first came;
Not a word had been spok'n, the past was all banished
  In manner withal no mortal can name.

TO LIZZIE.

Sweet Lizzie, love, at such a distance rings
  More like the memory of early dreams
Long since forgotten, which an idea brings
  Back to the real of remember'd themes.

Ah, Lizzie! did I love? I answer yes:
  Time only heals, it leaves a scar to tell
Of wounds inflicted, none may e'er guess
  The fair inflicter where she now may dwell.

The green grass covers perhaps her early grave,
  The cypress may sigh above her, the airy form
Be turn'd to dust, her soul to Him who gave—
  Leaving me hopeless to battle with the storm.

Mayhap she lives to gild another's life
  With rainbows of promise, of hope, and joy;
Mayhap she knew not the sweet name of wife:
  One point is known—I lov'd you when a boy.

THE SILENT LAND.

'Tis not the "Land of the Silent,"
  Silent to some it be,
For a Mother's hand, a Sister's voice
  Are beckoning to me.

I listen, I hear; oh, rapture!
  The song of the sav'd and free!
'Tis the joy of the just made perfect
  By blood of Calvary.

And strains of the sweetest of music,
  O'er the river float to me,
Like the voice of many waters,
  Like the surge of the restless sea.

A sense of the supernatural
  Dwells with me day and night,
And shows me the shining angels
  In robes of purest white.

And the whirr of wings angelic
  I hear in my dreams at night,
And a world of love and music
  Opes up to my ravish'd sight.

'Tis then that the sense supernal
  That dwells with me by day
Assumes all the shapes, the real,
  And soul forgets its clay.

METEMPSYCHOSIS.

TO LUCY.

The spirits of men, some philosopher said,
  Find a home after death in the bosom of birds.
But religion and reason have finally lead
  Us seriously to doubt the philosopher's words.

Yet if it were so, then my soul would desire,
  In winging its flight from this tenement frail,
To find its last home with the bird I admire,
  In the bosom of the sweet nightingale.

Then I could return on the wings of the night,
  From my home in the bow'r or grove,
And alight at her window in the gentle twilight,
  And sing to the spirit I love.

THE PEDAGOGUE'S SOLILOQUY.

Tho' Thomson said 'twas fond pursuit
To " teach young ideas how to shoot,"
Yet had he taught he had not wrote
Such language as above, we quote.
Talk of a doubtful suit at law,
Of being tickl'd with a straw,
Of hungry, waiting for your dinner,
Of courting one, but cannot win her,
Of bawling at a balky team,
Or paddling boats against a stream,
Of being witty without wit,
Of having clothes that do not fit,
A flea within your trowser's leg,
Of having doubts without a peg
To hang them on, an appetite,
With naught to eat from morn till night,
A scolding wife, a chimney smoking,
A dunce, a bore; Lord, how provoking!
A letter written, on a tramp
Thro' trunk and pockets for a stamp,
Mosquitoes, bed-bugs, flies and fleas,
Or aught unpleasant that you please,
Yet all in one will not portray
What teachers suffer ev'ry day.
First comes the little A B C,
With h-a and h-e he—-
And Bonaparte ne'er felt so big,
As these young heroes spelling pig,
Maguffey's series next appear
With pictures scatter'd there and here,
The urchins read wth stifled sound,
Like bees and insects buzzing round;
What see I next?   Alas, alas!

Smith's Junior English Grammar class:
"John is a verb of plural number,"
Young Socrates at once doth lumber,
"Of gender male, and it agrees—
May I go out, sir, if you please?"
Lord help with such a lot as these!
And as it goes take in account,
At all events, the vast amount
Of stock each parent doth invest
In Sook or Tom, the very best
That ever sat within a school
To go to sleep, or learn a rule,
Yet each one in their heart believing
Their sons and daughters most deceiving
At rapid learning. Mr. B
Peeps in each day or two to see
How John and Agnes get along,
And see that nothing's going wrong;
Says "Mathematics is John's forte,
We must restrain him, or in short,
He'll go distracted; little dunce!
He added up two columns once,
And since that time, why Mr. B
Says there's no *genus* such as he."
His Father asks in boyish glee
If he has reach'd the Rule of Three?
John answers quickly, eyes elate:
"I've cipher'd to the rule of eight!"
Precious youth from Heaven sent
To make another President,
Perpetual motion to invent.
Delightful task; yes, fond pursuit,
This teaching ideas how to shoot!
'Twere well enough, were it not true,
In doing so, they shoot at you.

COULD SHE WHOM I LOVE.

Could she whom I love for a moment know,
That her bliss was founded on another's woe,
The smile she wears and her voice of glee,
Would be ting'd with sadness as she thought of me,
When far away on a distant coast
To leave Thee, dearest, will grieve me most;
For Thou alone canst assuage my woe,
As thy blue eyes beam with beauty's glow,
As thy lips speak more than the utter'd word;
Aye, the sweetest music that I ever heard.
'Tis the soul that speaks, tho' the lips may move
And a heart that tells of its priceless love.
Tho' I met Thee the usual way—by chance,
That hour gave birth to the sweet romance
Of love in a moment, and yet sincere
As if I had known thee for a year.
I have pass'd the age when heart could sigh
For the beauty only of a face and eye;
I have pass'd that age when another's face
Could change my heart in a moment's space;
I have pass'd that age when a pretty eye,
Or a rosy lip, or a seeming sigh,
Could win me away from my destiny,
Which is all fulfill'd in my loving Thee,
The brightest being in this world to me.

CONTENTMENT.

How sad and cheerless is the heart
When hope and joy both depart;
When all its flowers, once so fair,

Do fade and leave a desert there;
When friendship's glow, and beauty's smile,
All lose their power to beguile?
The mad career of folly past,
The soul becomes serene at last,
No longer moved by passion's power,
When woe has wasted every flower:
'Tis then the restless spirit soars
Away from what it now deplores,
And feels as tho' the chains were riven
And breathes the native air of heaven.
Altho' I feel depriv'd of all,
The past I would not now recall,
For all its hopes were mix'd with fears,
And all its smiles preludes to tears.
Tho' I may gaze with fond regret
On all its buried treasures, yet
This heart, worn out with woe and pain,
Would not recall those scenes again;
But to its lot submissive bow,
And rather seek contentment now.

LINES TO ——.

Alas! it all my power defies
    To picture one so fair,
The beauty of whose beaming eyes
    Shines like a gleaming star.

A star! Can such a distant thing
    Vie with those orbs of blue;
Those mirrors of the mind which bring
    The soul to sparkle through?

Her glowing cheeks also possess
　The bloom of beauty rare,
With beauty shining none the less
　In her dark auburn hair.

Impassive hearts might gaze on thee,
　And only rev'rence feel;
I almost feel it would not be
　Idolatry to kneel.

But all have some attraction felt,
　However base and vile;
Methinks a Miser's soul would melt
　In sunlight of her smile.

PARSON PLEASE-ALL.

Parson P was a mystery
　Tho' not in the sense of witches,
His legs, they were not large, yet he
　Got "too big for his breeches."

He had been call'd, so we are told,
　To preach the gospel purely;
But bad sheep got into his fold,
　And he had to preach obscurely.

Now, Brother M., in front of him,
　Was no religious brother,
So in his texts he had to trim
　A path twixt "which and tother."
　Q

It would not do to go right through
　For M. would be offended,
And think, despite all he could do,
　He was the man intended.

But Brother P. was piously
　Inclined to straight-out preaching,
And "head nor tail," he once told me,
　Could make out of his teaching.

Result: he now began to bump
　His head against the pillars,
But found they were too hard a lump;
　These poor but pious fellows.

The pious man now hit a plan
　He thought would work divinely;
He'de preach to suit the upper clan,
　But treat the lower finely.

So he began with great clan
　To give an exegesis,
Such as Greek scholars only can
　When writing out a thesis.

And so his ministrations grew
　Exceeding efficacious
In soothing nerves of such as knew
　Their money-bags were spacious.

The parson could explain away
　The text about the needle,
That here, nor hence, no rich men play
　Upon the "second fiddle."

His church became the main resort
　Of easy-going sinners;
Not lewd ones, of the baser sort;
　The whales, and not the minnows.

In manner he was very bland
　To all the poor and needy,
And always lent an empty hand,
　Averring he was seedy.

And 'tis allow'd he should be proud
　At having such a choir,
While such a fashionable crowd,
　All parsons do admire.

He pitched his sermons on a plane
　Beyond all comprehension,
But silly folk were ever vain
　And fond of lofty mention.

Who but an ass, they said could sit,
　And contented to be fed,
On manna and the like of it,
　The real true gospel bread?

And so the parson grew severe
　On ministerial dullness,
By this his church throughout the year
　Was fill'd to over-fullness.

Each system of philosophy
　Was in its turn dissected,
How Huxley, Darwin, both could be
　By Scripture well protected.

And Aristotle and the like
  All came in for a share, sir,
Why thunders roar, and lightnings strike,
  How gas infects the air, sir.

He nearly prov'd that Balaam's Ass
  Was ridden by a Monkey,
And never had refus'd to pass
  Had he not been a Donkey.

Discourse no longer "cut and dried,"
  But spicy, sharp, and witty,
Including all things else beside
  The Saviour's love and pity.

Kind reader, now a moral draw
  From this disjointed story,
Of this weak man, who thought he saw
  A royal road to glory.

The truth, and nothing but the truth,
  Can win with saint or sinner;
You'll find this at the end, forsooth,
  And be a real winner.

What if a man should give offence,
  To few, where there are many,
He who will sit upon the fence
  Is not a friend to any.

Be what you are, cost what it may,
  If bad, strive to be better,
And never sell yourself for pay,
  Convictions to the letter.

And if you should be call'd to preach
Have but one aim in view, sir,
And never strive to overreach,
What God has bid you do, sir.

UNREST.

Alas, as here compell'd I sit,
I rack invention and my wit,
For some expedient which serves
To quiet my excited nerves.
It seems I have exhausted all
The sources that men pleasure call.
In early life I play'd my part
In serio-comedy of heart;
This folly o'er, I sought for bliss
In thousand other ways than this,
Became a student, poring o'er
Huge volumes full of garner'd lore,
Read novels, travels, by the score
Till surfeited, and read no more;
Next took to travel, thinking this
Would lead infallibly to bliss,
Until at length e'en change of scene
Became insipid, dull and mean,
When oft repeated; then became
Ambitious next to make a name
But soon, by observation, found
How soon is greatness underground,
Forgotten by the thoughtless crowd,
Who pipe in life its praises loud.
Amusements next; heard Patti sing,
And Nilsson make theatres ring
With plaudits, join'd the wild *encore*
Like all the rest, and call'd for more,

Until I thought, tho' thinking wrong,
How true the phrase, "not worth a song."

My next illusion to repair
To Halls of Congress, hoping there
To find excelling in debate,
Some hero from my native State,
But found alas, instead of it,
The low buffoon and vulgar wit,
And saw, with some excepted classes,
Our statesmen, Honorable Asses,
Instead of service night and day,
Thought only to increase their pay.
These men, at home from year to year,
On nothing live, yet have to spare,
Must have five thousand dollars here,
Or die of want—we dare to say,
None ever known to die that way.

What next: some fond and loving heart,
Devoid of deceit and art,
Not Fashion's fair and giddy queen,
(The heroine of a tasteless scene,)
But woman true, the richest gift
God ever gave to man to lift
His heart above the vulgar sway
Of low delights from day to day,
Whose cultur'd mind can both impart
The treasures of her head and heart,
Enthusiastic, not blase,
A toast upon a rainy day,
When bores and dunces cannot call
To stay an hour, yet stay all
With her, my Bible, books and friends,
Life sanctified by noble ends,
Thus spend our years, ten and three score,
In peace and write "Unrest no more."

TRUTH.

The soul of man, when forc'd to feel
　　Its utter vileness, stands aghast;
Naught from itself it can conceal,
　　The future only—not the past.

'Tis false that man believes a lie
　　He made himself, as some aver;
The soul is not the ear nor eye,
　　These do deceive, that cannot err.

" Yet language, as an art, conceals
　　Tho' giv'n on purpose to express;"
The poet, as he writes, reveals
　　Another's, not his own distress.

This is too deep for willing speech,
　　Which serves as porter to convey
Some selfish thought designed to reach
　　Its destin'd end and serve its day.

'Tis genuine tears and sighs express
　　Some traces of the unexpress'd,
A sea of feeling measureless
　　Pervades and fills each human breast.

Like exhalations, which arise
　　In silence, does the soul ascend,
And clouds in thought its silent skies;
　　Unseen by either foe or friend.

TO INCOGNITA.

Fair Lady, if we may believe.
　　The Fairies at our birth preside,
Each with their cup prepar'd to give
　　Some choice gift, 'tis not denied,

But that they gave with lavish hand,
　　The choicest that their cup contains,
To Thee: a presence to command,
　　And beauty which supremely reigns.

Impassive natures never feel
　　The bliss that beauty can bestow:
Such hearts are colder far than steel,
　　For e'en steel can melt you know.

How many balmy Sabbath eves
　　Unknown I've pass'd before your door,
And saw you sitting 'neath the eaves;
　　The type of beauty I adore!

Yet while my envious heart rebels
　　At seeing bliss I cannot share,
A blind fatality impels
　　My steps to wander where you are.

The secret passion I have nursed,
　　Despite what sense or reason says,
And what was but a spark at first,
　　Hath kindled to a lurid blaze.

Why should I hope?　Hope is a dream
　　At best and only, nothing more;
A light upon an even stream,
　　Which quickly dies when tempests roar.

Tho' I am not asham'd to own
  Aught that I love, and yet my name,
Address and place were better known
  To me alone, and that for shame.

I am a coward I confess,
  Yet beauty always made me so;
Love added makes my courage less,
  Therefore, I'm   Yours,

                                    INCOGNITO.

LOVE.

Oh, Love, tho' oft hath mortal tongue
Thy joys and thy sorrows sung,
Yet there are thoughts that 'round thee teem
Like shadows of a beauteous dream,
Thoughts no human mind may reach,
Defying ev'ry form of speech.
'Tis said, and credence must be given,
Prometheus filch'd its fire from Heaven.
Love giveth life to deaden'd hearts,
The sun of being that imparts
To ev'ry faculty and sense
A strength and power more intense,
Enlivens wit, makes fancy pure,
Imagination chaste, to soar
To brighter worlds by far than this,
Where it can consummate its bliss.
As lesser planets of the night
From greater all receive their light,
So love, the centre; aye, the Sun,
Shines for all hearts, refusing none
Who deign to bask within its beams,

Its light, which but from Heaven streams.
Oh, Love, the source of all that can
Expand, refine the soul of man,
Breathe thou but once upon my verse,
And that shall charm a Universe!
Words have no soul till love imbues,—
Without it, but the mind's refuse.
Love! Heaven's highest gift to man,
Eternal source whence God began,
The hidden links that sweetly bind
Created, with Eternal Mind,
The law of life, the central Sun,
The Light all worlds depend upon!
But touch my lips with hallow'd fire,
My song, like some celestial lyre,
Resounds through all succeeding ages,
Outliving lore of loveless sages
Till it shall mingle with the strain
Of bliss, when Hell and Death are slain.

ALTHO' MY HEART MAY STILL BE MOVED.

Altho' my heart may still be moved
  At sight of wo and pain,
Yet never more, in all its depths,
  Can it be stirr'd again.

There is a calmness in despair,
  A peace when hopes are wrecked,
The calm that fills a human soul
  Which ceases to expect.

SKEPTICISM.

Tho' atheistic spirits sneer
And call the earth disjointed sphere,
And seek to prove that ev'ry world
Was all from chance or chaos hurled,
In Nature's volume strive to find
Some proof that matter causes mind ;
That this ethereal essence springs
From " course fortuitous of things."
Such argument, to say the least,
But ends in proving man a beast.
The converse, then, of course ensues,
That beasts are men, you cannot use·
This argument with much effect,
So long, at least, as you suspect
Yourself a man ; 'tis all, you see,
A riddle of absurdity.
Mine be the easier task to find
In all, the All-Creating Mind,
In sun, and moon and planets see
Design, their name for Deity ;
For ev'ry atom, plant or flower,
Are tokens of creative power,
The smallest insect that can crawl
Attests the hand that made us all.
And, sneering atheist, can you tell
Who taught the bee to make its cell ;
Or who the beaver prescience gives
The hut to build in which he lives ?
Could chance do this, then chance must be
Another name for Deity.
Ye mighty planets that do pace
Your noiseless rounds thro' realms of space !
Ye tell me each nocturnal hour

A lesson of creative power,
Whose bare suggestiveness outweighs
All arguments that atheists raise;
But when mine eyes within but turn,
Where thought and hope and joy yearn,
Great God, alone in this I see
And feel an essence sprung from Thee!

FAREWELL, FOR THE WORDS THOU HAST SPOKEN.

Farewell, for the words Thou hast spoken,
  Each tie of endearment did sever,
And the spell that has bound me is broken,
  And its power hath vanish'd forever.

Thou hast treated the heart that I gave Thee
  As a thing that is worthless and vain,
Aye, the heart that would perish to save Thee
  Thou hast given to the cold world again.

Yet parting, I do not abhor Thee,
  Unfeeling and false as Thou art,
For the heart that was late beating for Thee
  Could not act so inconstant a part.

Again the wide world is before me,
  With its beauties that dazzle the mind.
And I who so late could adore Thee,
  My joy in another shall find.

I will now seek a heart that is beating
  In unison sweetly with mine,
Whose love is not changing nor fleeting,
  Nor false, nor so cruel as thine.

IN MEMORIAM.

The Husband of this lady was slain in her own yard, during the war, in the presence of herself and an only child by a detachment of Sheridan's Cavalry.

'Tis said, and time approves it so,
That human bliss foreshadows woe—
That when we feel relief from sorrow,
We may expect a dark to-morrow,
Ah! human life is wholly made
Of light and darkness, shine and shade ;
Where hope, like some resplendent star,
A moment shines with beauteous glare,
And then to us refuse its light,
At once obscured by rayless night.
It is this brotherhood of woe
That binds all human hearts below ;
That knits them as it were in one,
The only kindness woe hath done.
But there are pangs untamed by age,
Which earthly friends cannot assuage.
Sweet woman, deem not Heaven unkind,
Altho' its ways to thee are blind :
Ear cannot hear, nor eye can see
What God may have prepared for thee.
Then, lest thy feeling heart should break
With pain, 'tis best thou shouldst forsake,
And look beyond thy sighs and tears,
At all thy happy, smiling years
You spent with one, ere doom'd to part,
The keeper of your hand and heart,
Before his manly form was laid
To slumber with the nameless dead.
R

Oh! look beyond the dark abyss,
That now divides thy former bliss!
We know the human heart is prone
To mourn a loss it deems its own,
And if there be one earthly spot,
Where human nature is forgot—
Where feeling, pure as those above,
It is the grave of buried love.
But, ah! how swift, by mem'ry's power,
Is brought to view thy darkest hour,
When he that made thy life so sweet
Was slain, was murdered at thy feet!
Methinks I see the ghastly wound,
That pour'd his life's blood on the ground,
And hear his only fair-hair'd child
Pour forth her heart in accents wild—
Can see the demon troop who stood
And coolly shed her Father's blood,
And yet regret, when they are gone,
They had not slain and shed her own.
The heart, when long inured to woe,
May even cold and callous grow—
May smile at hope and be elate,
Nor fear no more the shafts of fate.
But there are wounds we all must feel,
Which cicatrize but never heal,
When fate, by one fell, cruel blow,
Hath slain our sweetest hope below.
Such were thy feelings on that day,
When he you lov'd was snatched away—
Torn in an instant from thy side.
Oh, death! couldst thou have not denied
So dread, so dark an hour as this,
To put an end to earthly bliss?
He is at rest—ah, weep no more,
The strife, the turmoil now is o'er!

Remember, could he hover near,
To see thee and his darling here,
To see them wretched would but pain
His heart, were it to feel again.
Above his dark and narrow bed,
Sweet flowers now their fragrance shed;
The dews of night, which seem to steep
The eye of Heaven, for him weep,
While every leaf that's swept by air,
Will breathe him a sweet requiem there.
Remember, too, that God hath given
To us our richest gifts from Heaven,
And if he takes them back again,
'Tis wrong that we should still complain;
And thou, his sweet and only child,
Remember while in death he smiled,
And would have press'd thee to his heart,
Wherein thou hadst so large a part,
Think of the last sweet words he said
To thee, ere death had o'erspread
The trembling lips so often press'd
By thine, when in his arms caressed.
Adore that God who hears on high,
The widow's and the orphan's cry;
Though of thine earthly father 'reft,
That God, your Father, still is left.

THE HYPOCRITE.

We know him by his drawling speech,
And by his aptitude to teach
The sterner lessons of the law,
As if all life were "bricks and straw,"
Puts on an elongated face,

When ever seen in public place,
His leaden lips always comprest,
As if in sorrow, or distrest,
In holy horror blinks his eyes,
And counterfeits a mock surprise,
When other's sins, less than his own,
Become, in course of events, known;
With a peculiar unction prays,
And takes good care that all he says,
When crowds are present, shall be heard,
That none may lose a single word,
Drops in the money—part of all,
He "robb'd from Peter to pay Paul."
If you but differ from his views,
The wretch no temper has to lose,
A heart of ice, a face of dough,
The sneak no friendship can bestow,
With none perhaps, except his wife,
Was ever angry in his life,
Brings up his children to believe,
The end of life is to deceive,
Nor known in all his life, by half,
The joys of an honest laugh,
No heart that can with pity melt,
And never indignation felt.
Ne'er feels aggrieved in all his time,
Except when caught and known in crime,
Then raises such a piteous yell,
One would believe the wretch in Hell,
Convicted, sneaks away to shun
The life he brought disgrace upon.

Poor fool! you make the Devil laugh,
Who knows too well, that even half,
The trouble, for deception given,
If rightly us'd, secures you Heaven;

You make yourself as miserable
As you can this side of Hell;
Your very faith and doctrine teaches
A wretched life and sour speeches,
Suspicion steals your peace of mind,
An acted falsehood makes you blind,
Men know you well altho' you rant,
In solemn, sanctimonious cant;
Your prayers, tho' long, cannot prevail,
They are best a lying tale.
Of woes unfelt : How can you dare,
To lie to God, engag'd in prayer ?
An open sinner's chance outweighs
Your own, when comes the Day of Days.
A coward, liar, sneak, and thief,
A servile spy, and not a chief,
You hold the vilest office yet
In all of Satan's cabinet,
Yourself, you to the Devil sell,
To do the lowest work of Hell.

YOUTH.

Alas! sweet days of early youth,
Bright days of innocence and youth!
Before my skies were overcast
With passion's storm or sorrow's blast,
Before I knew the ways of men,
More so, my own inherent sin,
Ere gall, and worm-wood, and deceit,
I tasted in life's cup so sweet,
Ere a reproaching conscience stung,
When only Pleasure's syren sung
A strain to lure me to delight

That left no bitterness or blight,
Before remorse, with bitter pangs,
Was fasten'd in my heart, like fangs
Of serpent, only to destroy,
My life, my bliss, my hope, my joy,
Ere love had thrill'd, with sense of pain,
Ere thought had come to tax my brain,
When hope could die and live again,
Within an hour, and the last
Bright as the one an hour past.

At times I see the babbling brook,
Upon whose banks I often took,
Such deep delight with line and hook!
At other times, the dear old pond,
Of which my comrades were so fond!
Unclad, upon its banks we gave,
Our bodies to the limpid wave,
Swam here and there with boyish glee
And "duck'd" each other with the spray,
Imaginary battles made,
And calling comrades to our aid,
We therw from our appointed place,
The fluid in each other's face.

At times I'm in the dear old school,
The rigid teacher with his rule,
And casting glances deem'd *incog*,
At pupils, whom he wish'd to flog.
I see again the sainted face
Of Mother, and the smiles that chase
Each other as her tender heart
In all our gambols took a part
From love and sympathy alone,
Which made again these sports her own
Which she knew well she had outgrown.

I see my Father, too, when he
Caress'd me on his welcome knee,
Told me how Giant-Killer Jack,
Huge burdens carried on his back,
How he, by cunning, strength, and skill,
Did match and other monsters kill,
Or told me of the wondrous sights
One reads of in Arabian Nights,
Meanwhile my wonder-waiting mind
Begg'd more descriptions of this kind
Till bed-time came, when Mother led
Me gently to my little bed,
And taught me, ere I went to sleep,
My little prayer, that God would keep
My soul until I should awake,
Or dead, that He the same would take.
But Mother, Father—both are gone,
And I am left, alas! alone.

DEATH.

INSCRIBED TO A MELANCHOLY FRIEND.

Sans doute, an entertaining thought,
Is surely his disease, has brought
The final reckoning to pay,
Put off of course till the last day,
If rich, how seedy relatives
Have but one fear, and that he lives,
Provided that his will bestow
On those who now lament him so,
That debt by all mankind pursued—

We mean the "debt of gratitude,"
And which, we notice by the way,
Few men were ever known to pay ;
If blest or curst with poverty,
Glad to get rid of such as he,
Conceal their joy none the less
By sniveling in mock distress,
And make your funeral's cost a plea
For paying debts some other day.

Blest with a pretty wife perchance,
Already in whose roguish glance,
Tho' dimm'd with tears, the secret fear,
She may not marry in a year,
And turn your tender children over
To the control of her new lover,
Who often does, (this may be hearsay)
Spank right and left and without mercy.
So my sad Alpheus, do not trouble
Yourself about your life—a bubble ;
Live right, nor be concern'd about
The manner of your getting out,
Take this to heart, which I now give,
"No death to those who truly live,"
Dismiss blue devils and such things,
Disorder'd stomach always brings,
Thy liver cleanse by exercise
And bid farewell to gloom and sighs,
Take all of Holy Writ to heart,
Nor dwell on some disjointed part
Out of connection, which would shake
The faith of martyrs at the stake ;
Do this, and I will pledge my word
Your groans will be no longer heard.

AIR CASTLES.

A dream of beauty! What else is human life:
For picture yours to the remotest span,
Strip it of phantasies, what else but strife
⁻ Marks ev'ry period from infancy to man ?
The swaddled infant pipes its feeble cries,
Prophetic of a life of tears and sighs.

Men philosophize, but philosophy
    Doth make us yet more miserable still:
It takes the scales but from our blinded eye
    To see the wide vista of human ill.
Heaven-born genius doth not bestow
Exemption on any: our lot is wo.

Childhood hath its pains; let poetasters
    Sing a delight no genuine bard hath known ;
Life from the first is freighted with disasters,
    The child hath sorrow the man's asham'd to own,
Trifles perhaps, and yet a broken toy,
As keen a sorrow as Priam felt for Troy.

The first attempts to walk, the thuds and knocks
    On hairless heads, the brainless, cruel nurse,
Who puts us down to walk upon the rocks,
    And if we cry, why then, so much the worse,
Put in a crib and tortur'd half to death
By tickling flies, or an infected breath.

Denied the sweet facilities of speech,
    We cannot damn them as we wish to do ;
But, turtle-like, lie on our backs and screech
    Till we are hoarse and almost frantic too,
Until our Ma, almost of love bereft,
By such mad yelling, spanks us right and left.

The cold neglect at each successive birth
  That follows ours, till forgotten quite,
Or strict constraint is put on all our mirth,
  For weary years in learning how to write;
Then taken home, perhaps to learn a trade,
And sweat on roads that Eve and Adam made.

We fall in love: what matter if we do?
  We cannot marry till a certain age;
And what young Miss has ever been so true
  As wait so long for us to tread the stage
Of young *beaudom?* If any, few there be,
And these, alas! we read about; not see.

Suppose she does, what difference does it make;
  We run a risk, a fearful one at that,
Our angel sweet another shape may take,
  Prove a cross between a tiger and a cat;
Or, put it milder, he may be forsooth
A Boaz, she—why anything but Ruth.

If otherwise, can we avoid our share
  Of ills and aches, the wretchedness we feel,
From want of love, when eating ill-cook'd fare,
  With buttonless pants, and socks without a heel,
Or shivering at night when cold Boreas blows,
Without a wife (a rug) to warm our toes?

Air-castles was our theme. Where are they now?
  Departed from us never to return!
To that false goddess we no longer bow,
  And for illusions we no longer yearn.
Perhaps, who knows, in worlds to which we go
They may return; be real all! We hope so.

LINES TO E.

When blighted in hope and baffled in zeal,
With all the keen anguish my spirit can feel,
Condemn not, sweet Lady, if I seem too severe
Or rail at some things I was taught to revere,
Condemn not, but pity, the spirit that feels
A sorrow whose keenness no language reveals,
And deem not its follies as a reveller's are,
But the phrenzy which seizes a mind in despair;
Could you know of the tempest that tosses my heart,
That wrenches its tendrils and fibres apart,
Not folly, but madness, not appearance, but pain.
Evokes such a tumult, supreme in its reign.
Still your sympathy proves it, and makes me believe,
That Friendship is real, though Love may deceive.
Kind Heaven hath bless'd Thee with a spirit to know
All the anguish refined of poetical woe;
Tho' the gift of expression may never belong,
Yet Thou art a Sister in the heaven of song.
Alone in Thy presence, can I wholly forget
All stars which before have arisen and set,
For who in the light of thy loving, dark eye,
Would mar the sweet present with a past agony !

MUSIC.

Sweet solace of an idle hour,
What mortal has not felt thy power?
And when thy gentle numbers swell,
With sweetness language cannot tell,
Who is not tempted to advance,
And join the pleasures of the dance?

O'er all the wide and warring earth,
Thou art a source of joy and mirth.
Thou drivest gloomy thoughts away,
Especially on a rainy day,
When murky clouds and patt'ring rain
On housetops keep a dismal strain;
When it is left for us to choose
Which we will have—thee or the blues.
Sweet solace of a soul in love,
Thy origin was from above.
The man of wealth and lab'ring swain
Are soothed by thy bewitching strain.
E'er since that holy man of old
Struck high thy notes on harp of gold,
The little bird and busy bee
Are found all imitating thee.
And in the blissful seats above,
Thy notes record that God is love;
While erring man thy notes beguile,
And makes thee serve a purpose vile.

UNWRITTEN SORROW.

Oh! there is a sadness not vented by tears,
When a moment embraces all the anguish of years:
We then feel a sadness too deep to be told,
A tumult of feelings no mind hath controlled.

It does not come as a wave o'er the rock,
But like the swift light'ning in its with'ring shock,
Which scorches all things in its fiery path,
Like a spirit of evil or the genius of wrath.

Did it come o'er the soul as a wave o'er the sea,
The heart might forget and again could be free;
Did it die on the soul as a sound of the lute,
Then its anguish for years we might not compute.

Like a bolt, it will blast what it cannot destroy,
Making barren the soul of its flowers of joy;
While the lustreless eye and the deep furrow'd cheek,
Tell a story more fearful than language can speak.

MY MOTHER.

There is a flower that cannot perish
In memory's urn, while I shall cherish
The thought of each remember'd joy,
Thy love to me, thy wayward boy,
                              My Mother.

My truest friend thou long hast been,
Who warned me from the paths of sin,
And when at manhood's prime arrived,
Still of thy counsel not deprived,
                              My Mother.

Till she has passed away from earth,
There's none can estimate her worth;
With none to hearken to their call,
And feel they are bereft of all,
                              Their Mother.

With none to soothe his boyish fears,
What voice to him as sweet as hers?
When death the dearest tie has riven,
I hope to meet again in Heaven,
                              My Mother.

S

ACROSTIC.

F air as a lily and sweet as a rose
A nd lovelier, by far, than either of those;
N ot given to vanity, pure as a child,
N imble and joyous, without being wild ;
I n the clear sunny depths of thy soul-telling eyes,
E nchanting sweet dream of happiness lies;

E nrapturing the vision permitted to view them,

B y the angel-like glances that scintillate through them;
O h, language! how feeble for utterance given,
W hen the soul is surcharged with the beauty'of Heaven';
E nfeebled and weakened with its feelings of bliss,
N or given the power to portray you, " Sweet Miss."

TO A FRIEND.

Dear friend, these lines are intended
　Alone as a token to thee ;
I wish you to take them and keep them
　Always in remembrance of me.
O, keep them as a pledge of that love
　That still in my bosom shall burn,
While life shall enliven its flame—
　Till my body to the dust shall return.
And when the frail body lies sleeping
　In the peaceful repose of the grave,
You will think of him who once lov'd you,
　And of this as the token he gave.

TO MATILDA, THE POETESS.

Thou bid'st me seek among the flowers,
In shady wood and tangled bowers,
Where wood-nymphs hold communion sweet,
Within their dark and lone retreat,
To find a gift which God has given—
Poetic fire sent from Heaven.
When prompted by poetic fire,
Thou mayest, I grant, to woods retire;
For babbling brook and balmy air
May kindle inspiration there.
But, ah! no power can control
Or check the language of the soul.
It breathes in the secluded glen,
Or 'mid confusion's angry din,
Where birds their dulcet numbers pour,
Domestic ease, or ocean's roar.
The soul, impregnant with its fire,
Needs not externals to inspire.

SABBATH EVENING.

Blest Sabbath eve, thine hours are given,
To muse on holiness and Heaven;
To leave the giddy world behind,
With all that may disturb the mind;
And leave the grosser joys of sense,
And soar to that pure region whence
Descends the balm which soothes the soul,
And makes the wounded spirit whole.
My heart once sought for every bliss
Afforded in a world like this,

'Mid crowds where mirth and beauty met,
To banish care—subdue regret.
'Twas vain; nor mirth nor beauty's power
Could cheer me in my gayest hour.
Altho' at times my feelings flowed,
And not one trace of grief I showed,
Yet still, within, some secret power
Would call to mind my dying hour.
Thou knowest not when death is near,
Nor when the monster will be here.
Alas! this world can never give
That which we sigh for while we live.
Teach me this wholesome truth to know,
How frail are all things here below.
And may its light be ever near,
To check me in my wild career;
Though fresh in youth and manhood's bloom
My active limbs must soon consume—
Must lose their force and pass away,
And be resolved again to clay.

THOUGH FATE HATH DOOMED ME.

Tho' fate hath doom'd me to forego
The bliss I fondly hoped to know;
Tho' sorrow deep from me hath wrung
The bliss the syren fondly sung;
Yet, dying, I shall leave behind
Some fruits of the immortal mind.
And tho' I ne'er can hope to soar
The heights of song, as some of yore,
Yet song alone, in darkest hour,
Can soothe the soul with magic power.
This be my solace while I sing,

And make me loath each sordid thing;
For naught on earth but chaste desire
Should ever prompt poetic fire.
But disappointments, dark and deep,
Awake the fires which sometimes sleep;
And, like volcanic Etna's breast,
Flame out more fiercely for their rest.
I would I were of placid mould,
Of impulse neither hot nor cold.
Then I could look on joy or pain,
Nor feel the throes I've felt again.
But till I drink of Lethe's stream,
The past will torture with its dream.

NIGHT, (IN THE CITY.)

Alas, how like my life the night,
That hides the city from my sight,
Save where some artificial light
　　Reveals the dim outline
Of murky objects which appear
Like horrid monsters such as leer
　　Their forms above the brine.

The churches' tall and slender spire,
In darkness lost, but serves to tire
The eye that vainly would aspire
　　Its utmost point to scan,
Too like, alas, the vain endeavor
Of mind, to pierce the far Forever,—
(Tho' baffled always, yielding never)
　　The destiny of man.

The prattle of the booted feet,
On thoroughfare and stony street,
Urged by some silly wish to meet,
   A sweetheart or a friend,
Are like desires that do tread
Incessantly thro' heart and head,
By impulse, and at random led
   To no specific end.

The streams of artificial light,
That flood each window late at night,
Are like the hopes that us incite,—
   These artificial too.
Within are forms of beauty rare,
Made so by glamour and by glare,
Appearing sweeter than they are,
   To superficial view.

The ball-room's gay and giddy crowd,
With music, mirth, and laughter loud,
Whose costumes are too oft a shroud,
   By means of heat and cold,
Now float before me in the light
That chandeliers will make at night,
But pains to think that such delight
   Will early make them old.

Give me the heaven's azure dome,
Where stars and blazing comets roam,
Seen from the porch of country home,
Where all creations endless tome
   Is open'd to my view ;
Where mind delights in vast display
Of myriad worlds and "Milky Way,"
Where night is sweeter than the day,
   And day is brighter too.

LAST WORDS

OF A YOUNG AMERICAN GIRL WHO COMMITTED SUICIDE, BY DROWNING HERSELF, IN LONDON.

The circumstances attending her death were these: She had been employed as Governess in an English family, and having lost her situation, with only a few pence in her pocket, she wandered through the streets of London seeking employment and finding none. She was very beautiful, and was therefore subjected to the most brutal suggestions, which she repelled with scorn. At last, when all her money was exhausted and there was only one alternative—shame or death—she chose the latter. A letter was found upon her person, to her Mother, in America, containing the sentiments expressed in this poem.

"I am far from those who love me,
  In a bleak and barren world;
With a frowning sky above me,
  And hopes in ruin hurled.

I've not a friend to pity
  And none to sympathize,
Tho' in the teeming city
  Where thousands meet my eyes.

Fatherless and motherless,
  Not a penny, nor a friend,
Death is my only fortress,
  Self-murder is my end.

The dark and rolling ocean
  Howls pitiless between
Each scene of love's devotion,
  Aye! each familiar scene.

I scan the stranger faces
  Which pass me in the street,
And seek in vain for traces
  Of love I never meet.

I am treading, slowly treading,
  With low and bated breath
The path inviting, leading
  Me to the bridge of death.

And now I stand upon it
  And gaze into the water,
Wondering if my Mother
  Sees the anguish of her Daughter.

Death is my only portion,
  Or lead a life of shame,
How can I, while devotion
  Shall last for Mother's name?

Oh, God! my refuge, hear me,
  Ere I make the fatal leap
Into the river, near me,
  Into everlasting sleep!

Forgive me, oh! forgive me,
  My present and my past,
A deed that must outlive me
  In the life aside I cast!

I have striven, vainly striven,
  To circumvent my fate,
Yet none have power given
  To shun a certain state.

Time taught me ev'ry letter
  In the alphabet of woe;
I feel it would be better,
  No matter where I go.

My dizzy head is reeling
  With plenitude of pain,
The stream behind me stealing
  That I cannot cross again."

These were the words she uttered,
  As she leaped into the river;
The waves a farewell muttered,
  And closed on her forever.

MY BIRTH-DAY.

LINES WRITTEN JULY 29TH, 1872, DURING A STATE OF GREAT
DESPONDENCY.

Alone in the world, tho' in the dense city,
  Where thousands of gay hearts go fluttering by,
Solac'd by the tattle of the lovely and witty,
  Whose hours of pleasure unconsciously fly.

Far, far from my home and the beautiful eyes,
  Which are beautiful only as love in them beams,
My soul is consuming itself in its sighs,
  As it feels the departure of all its fond dreams.

While others are raving over fanciful ills,
  Or curse an existence all sated with pleasure,
They taste not a drop of the mixture that fills
  My cup of disaster without stint, without measure.

What solace or charm in a gain-seeking city
   Is felt by the needy, the life-sick and weary,
For money-less orphans, the objects of pity,
   With mortals whose watchword is "Let us be merry!"

Five years, each crowded with a tale of its own,
   Have elaps'd since I saw e'en a Sister or Brother;
Depriv'd of my Father: my Father is gone,
   To glory, I trust, with my dear sainted Mother.

In my chamber alone, in the stillness of night,
   My spirit flies forth to the ends of the earth,
Or mem'ry conveys me, with mystical flight,
   To the scenes of my childhood, nay e'en my birth.

Till I hear, as it were, e'en the first feeble cries
   That I utter'd, as wrapp'd in the cradle I lay,
See Father and Mother as they fondle the prize
   Of their mutual love. God pity that day!

I grow with my growth and revisit each scene
   Of my boyhood tender to the estate of man,
Am again in each spot where I ever have been
   Re-dreaming each dream and replanning each plan.

'Tis the mis'ry of the moment that drives me to this,
   From a present that leads to the brink of despair,
To joys once enjoy'd; 'tis a measure of bliss
   And relief from the burdens I presently bear.

I feel I am writing no fanciful sketch
   Of pangs adventitious, but fearfully true;
Not pangs of remorse that may torture the wretch,
   Whose crimes, in confession, are piercing him through.

But the wildness of phrenzy that maddens the brain ;
 That scorches the soul which has trusted in God,
That cries unto Him from the midst of its pain,
 And striving to love Him, as he uses the rod.

FIRST LOVE.

Can the young heart exert
  More than once all its powers ?
Are there springs in a desert ?
  Can a waste produce flowers ?

Can a streamlet still flow
  When its fountain is dry ?
Can a flower still grow
  When its essence shall die ?

Can an army be scattered,
  Yet forsake not the plain ?
Can hopes that are shattered
  Be cemented again ?

Can a flame be relighted
  When its fuel is gone ?
Or a love be requited
  When heart there is none ?

Can purest love ever
  To friendship descend,
When its sweet bands shall sever
  And be at an end ?

POE'S SOLILOQUY.

SUGGESTED BY READING AN ACCOUNT OF HIS LIFE.

"'Tis useless to struggle,
    To be poor is my fate,
To suffer with hunger
    And the horrible strait
That one must encounter
    Without money or friends,
To be brought to the level
    Of beasts—human fiends
Possessing no more
    Of man than his skin,
While the heart of a demon
    Is beating within ;
To be fed from the offal
    That rich men refuse,
The advertised charity
    Which they cannot use
To a better advantage
    Than the practice which brings
A purchas'd benevolence
    With superfluous things.
Such morceaux avail one
    But little below, .
When tortured with hunger,
    Tormented with wo,
As he bears the contumely
    Of insolent asses,
As he seizes each straw
    Of subsistence that passes,
For a fragile support
    From the bodily pain
That consumeth the heart,

That maddens the brain.
'Tis madness and folly
  Contending with fate—
Each day I am falling
  From hope to that state,
When restless ambition
  Shall spur me no more
To seek for preferment
  With the wolf at my door.
Poor, gifted, yet friendless,
  Without aid I must sink
In the gulf of my ruin
  E'n now on its brink.
Existence is darkened
  With a horrible spell:
What is it but shadow
  From a spiritual hell?
Each plan has miscarried
  That I ever conceived,
Each friend has deserted
  That I ever believed;
All aspects are saddened
  That ever seemed gay,
All hopes that have gladdened
  Have vanish'd away.
Ah, stream of sweet Lethe,
  How soon unto thee
Would I sink could I know
  My spirit were free.
Sweet Mother, who loved me,
  Seest thou from the sky?
Canst pity my anguish,
  Or heed to my cry?
When the roses of Summer
  Hang a penitent head,
As if they were mourners

T

At the graves of the dead,
I long to be with them,
A sharer of joy,
Sorrow never may sadden,
Sin cannot destroy.
If the prayer of a mortal
Be permitted above
I feel thou art pleading
For the child of thy love,
That his feet may be taken
From the mire and clay
Of sin, and his soul
See the light of that day
That revealeth the secrets
Of destiny, fate.
And why he should suffer
So much in that state,
When others around him
Were sated with pleasure,
And pass'd an existence
Of elegant leisure,
With all the rare dainties
That earth can afford
That are pleasant to taste,
Or sweeten the board.
Why heaven-born genius,
With powers immense,
Succumbs in the struggle
With dull common-sense;
Why the light of that spirit,
Which is kindled on high,
Should ever dare question
The God of the sky?
No more of complaining,
I sweetly resign
My existence to thee—
That problem is thine."

THE BELLE'S REVIEW.

" Well, well, as here confined at home
By rain I'll let my fancy roam
Among my beaux, and criticse
Them as they pass before my eyes,
Altho' I readily confess
I criticise them none the less
When they are present, yet forsooth
I think, but dare not tell the truth.
But now I'll jot them down just here
For my own use and without fear:
First, then, that sentimental chap
Heart full of love—head full of sap,
The sweep of whose gigantic powers
Is limited to birds and flowers,
Whose intellect scarce worries through
A sorry pun or billet-doux.
He comes to quote the sweet tid-bits
Of love-sick nonsense, coined from wits,
Who write such stuff to earn, when read,
A pot of gin and loaf of bread.
He comes at eight—begins at once
(Lord, how I hate a love-sick dunce)
To quote what Moore and Tupper wrote,
(He has a thickness in his throat,)
Says 'Miss, I know you like the book—
I mean of course Moore's 'Lalla Rookh,'
More so that part wherein he tells
Of flowers, birds and dear gazelles,
Who charm him with their sweet black eyes
Who when they come to know him, prize,
And love him, die;' a bagatelle,
I sit and listen, groan and swell
With indignation that the dunce

Has naught original for once. .
Gets up at twelve, puts on his hat
As though to go, tugs his cravat,
Till step by step he's at the door,
Says 'Miss, I know you love t'explore
The starry depths, celestial fire,'—
(The wretch, I vow I will expire
Unless he stops,) next indicates
How stars prefigure all our fates;
And last, when prose and flowing verse
And poems of the Universe
Are hateful to my mind forever,
He leaves, still thinking he is clever.

What next? Why here comes 'Dandy Jim,'
Majestically tall and slim,
With clothing so exact and fine,
With diamonds from Brazilian mine,
With linen faultless as the snow,
His hair well oiled and all aglow,
In middle parted like design
Had been to draw for once straight line,
His pretty vest and silk cravat,
His coat of cloth and beaver hat,
His costly kids and shining shoes,
His small ratan, which he can use
In parlor well as on the street;
See these, and Jim is seen complete,
A maiden's beau-ideal; but stop,
All maidens do detest a fop,
Unless their brains, like his indeed,
Will rattle in a mustard seed;
He comes at nine, begins to prate
Of balls that he attended late,
Says "Miss La Belle was sweetly dressed
In silk Parisienne, the rest

In silks and satins trimmed with lace
Valencennes, and danc'd with grace."
Regales one with such talk as this,
Until at length, 'Excuse me, Miss,
Upon my word I find I'm due
To dance a set with Miss Belle View,
At ten o'clock.' He goes at once
And I am left without—a dunce.

What next ? Here comes my heavy beau
With youth exhausted long ago,
Whose wealth, he deems, will win the day
And take my virgin heart away,
And he so homely that a sketch
I herewith give of this old wretch,
Whom Pa and Ma would make believe
The husband best I could receive.
Imagine to yourself a man
Some forty summers if you can,
Give him a form whereof might brag
An ordinary Brobdignag,
Give him a head that is no doubt
As bald inside as it is out,
Give him a face that like a book
No preface needs, since but a look
Half given at his ugly phiz
At once informs you what he is,
Invest him with gray bearded chin,
Supporting lips reverse of thin,
Give him a nose not aquiline,
Nor pug, nor Grecian, but, in fine,
Belonging to the nameless tribe
Of noses no one can describe,
Give him next an eye that lacks
The brilliancy of old beeswax;
Well, here he comes, " How do you do ?"

" Do as I please ; " not so must you,
Sits down at once upon a chair,
Looks at me with a vacant air,
And then begins to talk about
All earthly things, and yet leaves out
The one just then I think sublime,
What else, except the flight of time,
Bores me to death with loud guffaw
At wit no mortal ever saw
Except himself. I cannot speak
But that his sides begin to shake
With merriment, my sorriest pun
With him as good as number one.
He leaves at last; Lord, what relief
Is mine for once: but oh, too brief!
Now if this dunce should ever dare
To court me, sure I shall not spare,
But he shall find out to his cost
A chapter in "Love's Labor Lost."

What next ? Here comes my pretty beaux,
So irresistable you know,
With locks as glossy and as fair
As poets tell of Venus' hair,
His teeth as faultless, white as pearls,
Complexion fair as any girls,
A hand as pretty as my own,
His eyes as bright as ever shone,
Withal that lazy, languid air
Of manners easy and don't—care,
Yet with his beauty, must be said
Without an idea in his head.
In fact, he is a piece of art
That charms the eye but not the heart.
He leaves at ten, good honest lad,
I thank him for the view I had

Of matter to perfection wrought,
Yet without one ennobling thought.

What next? My literary friend,
Whose tongue and talk are without end,
Who chats of books and men and things
Ad libitum, yet never brings
An idea down in all the chase
Before another takes its place,
He has all things at his tongue's end,
Except the patience of a friend.
This thought, it seems, with all he's read,
Has never once come in his head,
And yet so learned I much deplore
To call him—as he is—a bore;
Yet had his stay been premature
I had thought more of literature.

What next? Why "Fashionable Bill,"
Head full of schottische and quadrille,
Whose brains, if that his tongue reveals,
Not in his head, but in his heels,
The counterpart of "Dandy Jim"
Is all that I will say of him.

Who next, here comes the chosen one
Of my affections, never sun
Shone on a mortal half so bright
As he who owns my heart by right.
I did not meet him at a ball
Or opera, began to call
At first, companion to a friend
Who introduced, how it will end,
I cannot at this juncture tell,
For Ma and Pa don't like him well,
And yet I do, and they shall see

What comes if he prove true to me.
He comes at eight and stays till one—
Oh, how I suffer when he's gone!
His mind so full of pure desires,
He charms, delights, but never tires.
This ends the chapter: how I wish
Maids never did resemble fish,
That men could find aught else to do
Than angling for them and construe
Their actions in so wrong a light
As take a nibble for a bite,
For sure I scarce can be polite
To some acquaintances without
Implying love not thought about,
And yet alas I know too well
No lady can remain a belle
Who treats not each and every beaux
As if *the one* she meant to show
Her preference for, a sweet deceit
Kept up for admiration sweet,
And even now within my heart
I feel that I could never part
With any dunce upon my list,
And this perhaps makes me insist
Upon their coming, yet when done
I know I'll never love but one.

THE BEAU'S REVIEW.

" Well, well, as here confin'd at home
By rain, I'll let my fancy roam
Among the girls and criticise
Them, as they pass before my eyes,
Altho' I readily confess,

I criticise them none the less
When they are present, yet forsooth
I think, but dare not speak the truth.
Now women it must be confessed,
But differ only as they're dressed ;
Know *one*, some surly writer says,
And all the rest this one portrays.
This may be true, yet all the while
Each woman has a diff'rent style,
Their hearts however are the same,
In any country you can name.
But as experience, has been said
Best teacher mankind ever had,
I here propose for my own pleasure,
Near as I can to give the measure,
Of any fair one I have met,
And some whom I am meeting yet.

First then that amiable Miss,
Who ne'er objects to that or this—
Who gives assent to all you say,
No odds, how short or long you stay,
Bores one to death with tasteless tattle,
Of things not worth a baby's rattle,
Labors under infatuation,
That talk alone is conversation ;
Whose mind, if measur'd by her tongue,
Would surely kill a maid so young,
At last when patience is out done,
Tho' truth to say she's just begun,
And finding she makes no repentance,
Break off in middle of a sentence ;
Say, 'Miss, I'm sorry I must go,
Was up so late last night you know,
That I am forced my leave to take,
But none save you, have kept awake

Myself, so long and yet 'tis true,
I could set up all night with you,
You talk so well, but Miss good-night,
Sweet dreams and angels guard you right.'
The door is shut and out I go,
A walking monument of woe.

Who next? The maiden dignified,
Tho' lacking all things else beside,
And lacking this, but putting on
Because she thinks it will condone,
For other weaknesses which she
Deems greater sins than dignity,
Or else she does it thinking it
Creates sensation or a hit;
Expects to hear, of course denied,
'Why Miss you are so dignified,'
Talks in a cold and guarded way,
And never says, 'what did you say;'
Expects of course you will repeat
The question 'till she hears complete.
She thinks in her perverted pride,
Inquiring were undignified;
You cannot launch out into wit,
Or fun or humor, not a bit.
Talk by the card, that is to say,
Weigh every word you dare convey,
Till freezing process is complete
You leave and never wish repeat.

Who next? Why one who would resent
A kind word or a compliment,
Whose hobby is to criticise
All God ever put beneath the skies.
Thinks all men are 'not worth their salt,'
Disfigur'd by a single fault;
Whose mind is turned into a spy

For faults that may escape the eye,
The candid girl, whose chief delight
Is picking flaws from morn till night,
In all that she may chance to meet
In parlor, park, or on the street;
And yet while she no mercy shows,
Will not forgive the man who throws
Objection smallest in her way,
Until his very dying day;
She loves nobody, and thereby
No one can love her if they try.

Who next? The Fashionable Miss,
Whose motto is 'dry goods is bliss,'
Who never would have studied latin
Had she not found it rhymed with satin;
The only thing that e'er distressed her,
That at the ball some one out dress'd her,
A veritable female fop
Well known in ev'ry dry goods shop,
Where servile clerks in vain would shun her
And all seem loath to wait upon her,
Looks all the silks and satins through
And only buys a yard or two,
A mint of money runs to waste
For silks, yet never dress'd in taste,
A parent's darling, yet a curse
To one if minus a long purse.
I sit and listen to her chat,
Demurely as a tabby cat,
And never venture to advance
A single word except by chance
On any other subject than
The one most hateful to a man.
I leave her with a vague impression
That I am somewhat out of fashion.

Who next?   The female pleasure seeker,
Whose motto, aught except 'Eureka,'
Who lacking a contented mind
Has sought in ev'ry way to find
That bliss, which only one in seven
Has ever found this side of Heaven.
Your conversation does not hit
Her mark unless each word is wit,
Expects of course you will bestow
Immediate pleasure or else go.
For men she has no use at all
Who will not take her to the ball,
To concert, opera, theatre,
Where she can study human nature.
Expects her minister to tell
How infants crawl and cry in Hell,
How Heaven's gate stands open wide,
In short, all other things beside,
How Jesus wept and how he died;
Such subjects no excitement give.
She wonders how his people live
Beneath his plain and godly talk
Concerning Christian's life and walk.
At length you leave her in disgust
With an impression of mistrust
That you have bored her more than half
To death, and acted like a calf.

Who next?   Miss La Belle Hard-to-please,
Whose presence puts you ill at ease.
You cannot say the weather's fine,
But it is bad, she will opine;
You cannot compliment a friend,
A book, or aught by mortal penned,
But what she differs in a trice
And says 'your book and friend were nice

Were it not for grievous fault
That makes them hardly worth their salt ;'
Take any subject that you choose
You'd find it does not meet her views,
Until worn out with wish to please
You bid good-night and feel—at ease.

Who next? Miss of uncertain years
'Twixt Sylla and Charybdis steers,
The cautious mortal who would dare
To talk of certain subjects there,
Must shun allusions to the past,
Or else it does reflection cast
Upon her age—a tender spot ;
'Tis best with this to meddle not.

Who next? Why others I could name,
But variations of the same,
The Prude, the girl of period,
Girls that excel in bow or nod.
But I forbear and now proceed
To single out the few indeed   ,
Upon my list who do embrace
Some charms beyond a pretty face.

Who next? A maiden that can plead
No guilt to aught that I have said,
A woman true, no thing of Art,
Who has what few do have—a heart,
A mind so exquisitely planned
That all things seem at her command,
A wit so pure, so chaste, refined
Per force it pleases all mankind,
A presence too so chaste and sweet ;
In short, a being so complete
You can but think and wonder why
    U

The rest don't take their pattern by.
With her the wing'd hours fly
So sweetly, so unconsciously.
No sense of weariness or pain
Resulting from the dismal strain
That taxes ev'ry nerve, and brain.
To edify, when edifying
Is but a painful sense of trying.
The social cup does not contain
The lees, but nectar of the brain;
In brief, the heart's and minds' champagne
Is set before one as he sips
Her words—the service of her lips.

Who next? Of course the Chosen One,
The brightest being 'neath the sun,
Whose mind is of the classic mould,
Like heroine's in the days of old,
Would bear the torture of the stake,
Or rack, were it for conscience sake,.
A modern Roland who would die
On guillotine, than stultify
Her sense of right, no compromise
With tyranny e'en tho' she dies,
Contented with the nobler way
That only higher nature's sway.
Her brilliant wit's incessant flow
Like Sheridan's cannot forego,
Ignores the jargon of the schools,
Resource of non-creative fools
Devoid of wit, who would supply
'A sea of words to drown a fly.'
Her mind admits no common place,
Will not consent to join the chase
Of childish Fancy's butterflies,
So sweet to weaker maiden's eyes;

Enough, description she defies,
A task in vain to him who tries.

What now ?   Ah, well, to end it all,
There are maidens large and maidens small,
There are maidens dull and maidens bright,
There are maidens wrong and maidens right,
There are maidens bitter and maidens sweet,
All sorts of maidens to make complete
A world where bitter blends with sweet.
'Tis true there's more or less deceit
In social circles in which we meet,
But a little of this is not a sin
But virtue in woman 'thro' thick and thin,'
For candour that borders on cruelty
Is not so pleasant as one can see,
And the man aspiring to be a beau
Makes up his mind that he will eat crow
If the dish of Fashion but sanctions so.
The chapter ends; I must away,
And meet them all at the next *soirée*.

THE STORY OF AN OUTCAST.

"A few years; ah yes, a few years only,
    And I was innocent and guileless too
Then alone, God knows I was not lonely ;
    No one is lonely when their life is true.
My Father and Mother were all love to me,
I felt no fear of what I once should be.

Ah, happy years, charm'd with the guileless glow
    Of early joys, I trudg'd my way to school ;
No horrible phantom of my future woe

E'er shone upon me, but the even rule
Of woman's life to follow and pursue,
To love, to marry, as all others do.

A few years more, a woman I became;
   No, not a woman, but a blooming maid,
I need not here recite my fall, my shame;
   On base, ignoble man that crime is laid,
Man who with loving, lying lips hath cursed
Woman's best life, forsakes her in the worst.

Ah, could my cries in Heaven no pity find,
   Betray'd by man, does God forsake me too?
Ev'n Hell would be a refuge to mind,
   Foul as I am and living as I do,
Depending now alas for bitter bread
On such as launched this ruin on my head.

Oft, oft, in the lone watches of the night,
   When ribald songs and lewder jests all cease,
I live my life over, searching for the light
   Of other days, of joy, of love and peace,
And in sweet dreams my vileness all forget,
Unconscious then my sun of hope is set.

And yet I live in wretchedness and pain,
   Hate what I lov'd, and love what I should hate,
Drinking deeper, deeper, that I may drain
   My cup of poison, till pitying fate
Take me away a worn and blighted thing
Without one tear, one floral offering."

THE MORAL.

Ye moralists stern who never stirred
   At tales of human wretchedness, how far
Deem ye your mandates are known and heard

Revolving in orbits like some little star?
Men may be wiser, they never will be better
Whose hands are bound in so strong a fetter.

For youthful folly, ye can no pity feel,
    For indiscretion always have a sneer,
Style all fanatics who study human weal,
    And " bless the stars " because your skirts are clear.
Harlots in Heaven an easier access find
Than ye, than ye, blind leaders of the blind.

We know of one who leads a life of shame,
    Her youth was stainless, her young life pure,
The fell destroyer, the dark seducer came
    With tales of love, those arts that well secure
A maiden's ear, his heart was black as Hell,
She listen'd to him, and in list'ning fell.

And where is he, destroyer of her peace,
    Foul murderer! I write it to their shame
'Tis a mark of honor, smiles did not cease
    Foul as you are, yet still " creme de la creme!"
Could not afford to lose a shining light
Nor part with one whose vices were so slight.

WHICH ?

THE FIRST.

Is winsome, lithe and small,
Tho' Nature had exhausted all
Her finest skill to make complete
A body for a soul so sweet,
Her eyes, without a microscope
Seem little worlds, where love and hope

Are dancing ever, like the beams
Reflected from the limpid streams
Of thought so pure that one descries
Their beauty in her very eyes.

THE SECOND.

Walks the earth a queen,
As if the ground were far too mean
For her to touch, her brow and eye,
Reveal the seats of majesty,
Her sister she excels in size,
Unlike in feature, form or eyes,
And tho' her heart, like hers, refined,
Yet widely differs in her mind
One born as if her place, to hold
With Titans like the same of old,
Classic, heroically grand,
Aye born to empire and command,
While lips and mouth, and chin and nose
Mind, will and resolution shows.

THE FIRST.

Is exquisitely sweet
In manner and her soul replete
With kindest sympathies and love,
For all around her and above,
Can weep and smile and sigh and sing,
And from our souls extract the sting
Of woe, and heal the wound and smart
By love—the honey of the heart,
Her soul is like her form and face,
All beauty, comeliness and grace,
A mind and eye that beauty sees
In all things, therefore BORN TO PLEASE.

THE SECOND.

In manner, as in form,
Will brook, not bend before the storm,
Yet forces in resistless way
The heart its utmost tribute pay,
Nor scarcely deigns to look upon,
With pride, the triumphs she has won,
She crowds into, but will not twine
Around our hearts like eglantine,
But claims them as a right divine.
Ambitious and aspiring soul
That seeks, but will not brook control,
Which love I best, I cannot tell
But this perhaps will answer well,
Were one unknown, the one I knew
Would have it all, without ado.

[PUBLISHED BY REQUEST.]

THE AUTHOR'S FIRST ATTEMPT AT RHYME.

Not very long since, being invited to dine,
At the house of a friend, yes an old friend of mine,
To partake of his meats, his fowls and his stews
Was hard, very hard, for me to refuse;
So making arrangements my toilet, and dressed,
I mounted my steed by no means the best.
But I'll give a description, so that you may see
What a rare piece of horseflesh most truly was he.
His hips stood out like the legs of a table
While his ribs you could count as he stood in the stable,
His ears, which were long, were as stiff as a block,
And flapped at each step as true as a clock,
His voice, at times, tho' remarkably strong,

Was almost as sweet as a nightingale's song;
At times, in the middle, 'twould gradually swell
With a sound like the gong at a country hotel.
When pulled to the left he'd go to the right,
And squall just as certain as a house came in sight,
Which set all the turkey's and guineas to squalling
While the mules in the stables would answer his bawling.
From this short description you may readily see
He could cure the worst cases of chronic *ennui*,
But I rode on admiring the beauties of nature
And paid no attention to the fuss of the creature,
I was charm'd with the beauties of sweet solitude,
And thinking of feasts when the appetite's good.
Oh, sweet to my soul my reflections just then
When a stump came near ending the existence of " Ben,"
For the steed did his rider most viciously fling
While a wheel of locomotion to the stumps did cling.
The obstinate beast heeded not my commands,
But dragged me some distance along on my hands,
And while the poor rider was gaping for breath,
The wretched old Mule tried to kick him to death:
Had one of his hindfeet but hit on my head
This rhyme you're reading would have ne'er been read.
At least I don't know how the event might be,
But one thing is certain, ne'er written by me.
Sir Mulee agreed at length for a truce,
I improv'd the kind offer to get my foot loose.
The animal then turn'd and haughtily neighed
As if to rejoice o'er the wreck he had made,
Then bounded away like a deer o'er the fields,
And my patience tried sorely while trying his heels.
He shaped his course through a deep tangled wood,
And I followed behind him as fast as I could,
The undergrowth howe'er which smote in the face
Was quite a pullback, as you know, in a chase;
With the slashing of bushes and the breaking of sticks,

A medly of sounds did at once intermix.
Now mind you, a fence lay plump in the way ;
Ah! there, Sir Mulee, I'll bring you to bay.

How sad feels the heart when hope disappears,
When the castles all tumble which fancy uprears !
I thought of this stronger than I e'er have since
When the crazy old Mule jumped o'er that fence.
Tho' I'de hardly the heart to follow him on,
But I saw his pathway was blocked up with corn,
I thought the temptation would bring him to halt,
And knew if he did'nt 'twould not be his fault ;
But he heeded it not and pressed on with speed.
Oh, how my poor heart was again doom'd to bleed
When I saw that he heeded neither fences nor feed !
Now mind you, this happened in the hot month of June,
When an egg could be roasted in the sunshine at noon,
The warm perspiration came out in a sluice,
Or trickl'd like the gravy when you roast a fat goose.
I've read in a book, or somewhere or other,
How lasting and pure is the love of a brother :
But, brothers or brethren, there never will be
Who could stick any closer than my shirt did to me,
My collar to my neck more tenderly clung
Than e'er did a babe to its Mother when young,
Soon totally vanish'd or lost all its shape, or
Became just as pliant as a piece of wet paper.
At length Sir Mulee came to a stand-still,
Where once stood a foundry and perhaps an old mill,
There I caught him again. (Great Heavens how hot !)
So altered and chang'd e'en the mule knew me not,
My very first thought was to kill him outright
As being the curse of my miserable plight.
Tho' all unaccustom'd I could have then sworn,
But reason prevail'd, so I let him alone.
The wages of sin shall be paid to the sinner ;

I certainly thought I had paid for my dinner.
Having mounted again, set out on my journey
With a business air like a clerk or attorney.
As my head came so near being hit by the steed,
I concluded at length I was lucky indeed,
At least in these days when so much of it's taken,
I thought I was lucky in saving my bacon.
Next was to surmise what prompted the Mule
To prevent me from gaining my Ultima Thule.
Did he deem me a preacher; then his motives were good
In spreading the gospel wherever he could.
Did he deem me an editor; then his motives were plain,
Since they fill up their stomachs by emptying their brain.
No wonder they are lean and much emaciated,
As they are bound to be hungry from reasons just stated;
For we know by experience that a keen appetite
Is not easily dull'd when the diet is light.
But fearing a lengthy digression will bore ye,
And wishing to be brief, I'll return to the story.
I deemed that my trials at length were all o'er,
Mishap I was certain would happen no more.
I'de forgotten to notice before I went down,
A pair of old socks hid in my hat's crown,
And being, as you know, in such a sad plight
I thought to atone by being polite;
Taking my hat off, I bow'd as I entered the door,
When the *darned* old socks roll'd out on the floor;
Some stared, some grinned, while a few seemed to pity,
Considering the subject more serious than witty,
But there I stood grinning like a young alligator
And feeling as cheap as an Irish potato,
Finally I took courage enough for a seat
By a lady I thought most winning and sweet,
The lady I talked to soon turned out to be
A mistress or maiden—either one did for me,
From her side I retreated with greatest celerity,
Well knowing the effects of a husband's temerity,

I was looking for him to come down on my head
"Like a thousand of brick," as some fellow said.
I related the joke to a dry looking elf,
When, lo and behold, 'twas the husband himself.
Believe me I tell you I felt much inclined
To give the old lady a piece of my mind
For the mistake she made when she gave introduction
Which came so near proving my total destruction;
But I let it all pass as a very good joke
And concealed all the fire in good humor's smoke.
These reflections however made me feel rather sour,
But just then the gong announced dinner hour;
In obeying the summons I an ink-stand upset,
Making the marble-top bureau at once pretty wet,
And fearing detection, that it might not be seen,
I pulled out my 'kerchief and wiped it up clean.
This being accomplished, I went into dinner
With about as much grace as any other sinner,
For a very short while all went on quite well,
To me it seemed only as a short breathing spell,
A lady sitting next me requested the soup,
I tried to comply by raising it up,
But some how or other, by chance or mishap,
I stumbled and pour'd all the soup in her lap.
To apologize then was all I could do,
When the married lady's dress caught under my shoe,
'Twas a sin to see how muslin and calico flew;
I pulled out my kerchief for my face all aglow
When lo! it became as black as a crow.
So I silently swore most bitterly then,
This trip is rather one too many for "Ben;"
Could have crept in a hole that a gimlet could bore,
Or sank to a grease spot right down on the floor,
So I pledged to myself right there and just then,
You will never hear more of the courtships of "Ben."
But a pipe and some primings I'll try to procure,
And smoke them and never go courting no more;

But set up a house which the ladies all call
A dirt-dobbers's nest or a bachelor's hall :
And meditate there on the trials of life,
But especially the trouble of getting a wife.
But I've already taxed your patience too long,
So I think it is high time to wind up my song,
And by way of concluding this lengthly epistle,
I think I paid dear, very dear, for my whistle.

POETIC DIFFICULTIES.

'Tis not so easy now-a-days
For one to win poetic praise,
Since ev'ry subject from a louse,
Or from a mountain to a mouse,
Is duly coated o'er with rhyme,
Or whitewash'd with poetic lime.
One cannot sing of Hope in measures
But that he's told of "Campbell's Pleasures,"
Nor in Imagination pride,
But what he meets an Akenside.
Immortal Milton! rest secure,
For weaker wings can never soar
Up to thine imperial height,
But lower peaks suffice their flight.
The days of sweet poetic dreams,
Pegassus spurring on his teams,
The Muse, the Nymph, inspiring song,
All to another age belong.
This is the golden age indeed
If gold mean nothing else but greed,
And railroad stocks suffice, at present,
To purchase ev'ry thing that's pleasant :
No more, they wear out heart and brain

To catch some bard's familiar strain ;
The midnight lamp now burns no more
In treasuring up poetic lore,
For money buys all this without
One's troubling much himself about ;
Five dollars will suffice to buy
A name to last you till you die,—
Distinguished, celebrated, noted,
Will in your praise be often quoted ;
A monkey-keeper, vagabond,
Whose name's with foreign title donned,
Is call'd the eminent professor
Or zoological possessor
Of secrets far beyond the ken
Of common, ordinary men ;
An editor, whose pasquinades
His columns every morn invades,
Be sure is now a real wit,
Self-made, withal, the best of it.

THE FOUR SISTERS.

SOME REMINISCENCES OF THE AUTHOR'S YOUTH.

I.

Not far from Blue Ridge base is seen,
Tho' Shenandoah brawls between,
So fair a spot that to my eyes
Seems like an earthly paradise ;
There ev'ry plant or flower that springs
Are pictures of Diviner things
Than roses sweet or lilly fair
That bloom upon the earth elsewhere.
V

II.

But 'tis not fields or flowers fine
Which makes that spot to me divine;
Ah, more than this, since it hath given
To me an ever-present Heaven,
A memory that a soul might crave,
Ere soaring to the God that gave,
And bless him as it soars on high
That such remembrance cannot die.

III.

'Tis love can change the darkest spot
Into an Eden, make the cot
A palace, make the bitter sweet,
Our life reverse and make complete;
'Tis love that gives to nature's face
Its beauty, comeliness, and grace,
Imbuing all with soul and spirit,
With charms dull earth cannot inherit:
The pearly dewdrop sparkling clear,
Is emblem sweet of beauty's tear:
The tints that streak the blushing rose,
When first its petals half disclose,
Are like to those that artists seek
To stereotype on beauty's cheek.

IV.

So is it with the blissful spot
Which ne'er by me can be forgot;
There first my young and ardent soul,
Then like to some unwritten scroll,
First felt, as if its God above
Had simply written on it, "Love."

V.

Four sweet and gentle sisters grace
This antique yet romantic place:
Edmonia first, whose face portrays
The brilliant mind in ev'ry phase
Of action, feeling, and the swell
Of fine emotion, one may tell,
While beams from out her lustrous eyes
Of brown, a speaking paradise.
Ah, may she long survive and be
As dear to others as to me.

VI.

Sweet Fannie next: Divinest Muse
Thy magic aid do not refuse,
Assist me now, as ne'er before,
While I my feeble numbers pour
In trembling verse upon the shrine
Of what I deem almost divine!
A lovely woman, all possest
Of qualities to make us blest.
Where less celestial ears and eyes
Lose all except the harsher cries
Of discord, agony and pain;
Her soul drinks in the deep refrain
That saints on earth and those above
All sing in chorus, "God is Love,"
And yet withal, (not oft below)
Appreciates a poet's woe,
Knows that the sweetest song he sings
He from a bleeding bosom wrings,
Knows that his heart requires more
To soothe it than the world's *encore*.

VII.

Dear Alice next our pen employs,
Whose image in my mind decoys
Our thoughts too far for us to show
What beauties from her image flow,
How meekness, gentleness, combined
Are pillars in her happy mind;
She, born to solace and caress
Man's spirit broken in distress,
Her soft, sweet voice hath power to heal
A spirit torn upon the wheel
Of fate, with it the innate power
Sufficient for the trying hour,
That true nobility of mind,
Which tho' it deem its fate unkind,
Yet turns within itself and sees
Resources there to give it ease.

VIII.

Now, last upon the list appears
A maiden sweet, of youthful years,
A lovely bud, a blushing rose,
Yet sweeter far than both of those,
Whose tender years give promise fair
That Loolah is destined to share
In all that's either bright or good
Pertaining to her sisterhood,
When calm maturity of thought
Has all her features finely wrought,
And added to the sweet expression
So fully now in her possession,
Those finer traces which arise
When first some cherished object dies,
That crops th'excrescences of hope,
And gives the reason wider scope.

AT FIRST SIGHT.

Sweet Maiden from that very hour
  I met Thee, I have never known
A moment's freedom from the power
  Thy charms around my heart have thrown

In vain I struggle to be free
  From Love's dominion; 'tis in vain,
I own, yet curse the slavery;
  Make link by link, yet hate the chain.

And yet I know that woman's heart
  Is never won by love alone,
And still when one assumes a part
  He cannot act till love be gone.

LINES TO A STUDENT.

'Tis written that Athena sprung
  With power from the brain of Jove,
And took at once her place among
  The gods upon Olympian grove.

In seats of learning, hid for years,
  The student busy night and day,
At length Athena-like appears,
  Full fledged and ready for the fray.

The school is but a training camp,
  The world is your true battle-field;
'Tis there the hosts of Error tramp,
  That Truth alone can force to yield.

'MID THE HOURS DEVOTED TO PLEASURE.

'Mid the hours devoted to pleasure,
 The heart may banish its pain;
But soon, in a moment of leisure,
 Does sorrow steal on us again.

The soul immortal is sighing
 For bliss it cannot obtain;
Though baffled, persists still in trying—
 Though repulsed, yet attempts it again.

The pursuit far exceeds all the pleasure
 Of real or fancied bliss,
For soon must the heart's purest treasure
 Decay in a dark world like this.

For a moment may bliss be complete,
 When the heart may forget all its woe;
But the bitter soon poisons the sweet
 Of the dearest enjoyment below.

NOW AND THEN.

It hath not been so alway; time hath been
 When I was better and holier than now,
Ere the drops that sparkle in the cup of sin
 Lent joy delirious, when my youthful brow
Felt the warm endearment of a Mother's hand
To soothe my young spirit by some shock unmanned.

It cannot last alway ; the turbid stream
  Of passion at length, must itself subside ;
Life hath more than one phase ; another form,
  Brighter and fairer, a smoother tide,
Ere long, shall waft me to a fairer shore
Where change, save for the best, shall come no more.

The siroccoes of passion wither ev'ry flower
  With deadly breath, yet giving in their stead
A brute existence, a longing to devour
  Our own hearts, a craving endless, tho' e'er fed
With sensual dainties ; 'tis an appetite
Which becomes but keener with each new delight.

'Tis a fearful thought that all our deeds must shine
  In the light of Heaven, visible to all ;
No hand can shield us from the eye Divine.
  For no arm can save us ; great, high, and small,
If guilty, covered with guilt must ever fly
From themselves in vain—the worm that cannot die.

THE UNWRITTEN THOUGHT.

There lurks a thought in every heart
  Refined from passions fire,
A thought that dwells, tho' unexpressed,
  With all till they expire.

Tho' mem'ries bitter as the sting
  Of death are rankling there,
Still this celestial thought can bring
  A solace in despair.

We feel it most when mercy's tear
Awakes to flow at pity's moan,
When others' sorrows we transfer
And feel them as it were our own.

We feel it when the heart forgives
What it has nursed in deadly hate
The blessed leaven that can give
A sweetness to the fruits of fate.

Angels alone its raptures know,
Tho' they alone its depths can name,
Still it exists where passions glow,
A spark of the celestial flame.

'Tis this exalts the human soul
Above the vileness of its clay,
Whose softest whisper can control,
And free the mind from passions sway.

WOMAN.

Oh woman, born to intersperse
With flowers the Universe!
To thee I bring my humble lay
A votive offering to-day,
And place it trembling on the shrine
Of what I deem almost divine,
A woman true, if false she be,
No lay nor line expect from me;
A woman false is both a curse
And plague to all the Universe.
In man we but expect to meet
Guile, envy, falsehood, and deceit;
But woman's sphere alone embraces

The territory of the graces;
When true, the brightest gift to man,
The hidden source whence love began.
Nor was it filch'd from Heaven's sky,
But shone the first in woman's eye,
When Eve, her Mother, first was given
To Adam from the hands of Heaven;
He saw it in her beauteous face,
In all its comeliness and grace:
So pure, so chaste, untainted then,
As now, with any trace of sin;
For love is power to impel
And make the heart of manhood swell,
To nerve its arm to deeds of daring,
To kindle hope when most despairing.
The poets most ecstatic dream
Is kindled by the radiant beam
That sparkles in her lovely eye,
When mind and soul and passions vie,
Which scintillate with living fire,
The thoughts that in the soul transpire.

MONEY.

Oh money, let me sing of Thee,
The only genuine friend to me,
I would not give thy meanest cent
For all the love that men invent:
For "what is friendship but a name,"
Some writer says, and love the same;
When sickness doth the chest invade,
'Tis Thou that lends thy magic aid
While scores of sympathising friends
Inquire if the patient mends,

And when the bloom of health returns,
The Doctor's joy is what he earns,
Not that the soul is in its socket,
But that the dimes are in his pocket ;
The Miller each nocturnal hour
Is praying for a rise in flour,
While Merchants vent a tale of woe
About each sale they made too low ;
The Bakers wish mankind were fed
Alone on cakes or baker's bread,
While Pedagogues their pupils thrash
Because tuition is not cash ;
E'en Priests and Prelates, now-a-days,
Confess Thou hast some winning ways,
Nor be convinced they have a call
If they but learn the pay is small,
While candidates for office use
The vilest language one could choose
About each other, seek to prove
To country their undying love,
Yet running by the peoples wishes
To office, for the " loaves and fishes."
How soon the patriot flame goes out
When money is no more about,
No care for honor at this day,
If that this honor does not pay.

Ah, would you know a friend is true ?
But ask him to endorse for you :
With what politeness he refuses,
What feigned looks and fair excuses,
And tells you oft, in saddest way,
" I hardly know how I shall pay
The note I have in bank to-day."
Ah, should you fall in love and yearn
To know how that your suit will turn,
Consult your pocket, it decides

The fate of all our modern brides,
And in your favor turns the scale,
As Byron says, where seraphs fail.

Oh, Money, I could sing thy power
Until life's last protracted hour,
At last, like Sheba's queen of old,
Exclaim "the half had not been told!"
For thee are worth and beauty sold,
And woman's charms laid out in gold.
In vain the weeping Daughter sues
For mercy; she cannot refuse
(Altho' for years she may have plead)
The parents mandate, and must wed
The liar, rake, inhuman brute,
And thus become a prostitute,
Yet parents deem that God will bless
A union of such wickedness.
Pause Woman! Ev'ry vow you tell
At such an altar rings in Hell,
Satanic laughter in the strain
Of wedding march, a funeral train
The dirge of ruined womanhood,
The death of all within you good,
While angels weep in realms above
For crimes done in the name of love.

Thank Heav'n howe'er this world affords
Some wealth beyond the miser hoards,
That there's some to whom is given
"A spirit less of earth than Heaven,"
Who live above the low delight
That filthy lucre can requite,
In place of love, whose riches live,
Beyond the grave, destin'd to give
That home which money cannot buy—
The everlasting home on high.

ROBERT E. LEE.

Virginia, synonym of all
That stirs the heart, on Thee I call
For inspiration such as given
To poets from a fabled heaven ;
And while the plains of Marathon
Are dear to ev'ry Grecian Son,
And bloody Austerlitz enhance
The glory of thy chaplet France,
And England, full of honors too,
Boasts of her dreadful Waterloo,
Let Athens claim Demosthenes,
And tragic Greece, Euripides,
England gifted Shakspeare claim,
And Milton of an equal fame,
Let France with martial joy own
Her unapproached Napoleon,
Still let me sing in humble strain
Virginia and her heroes slain.
Her mountain tops, that seem to kiss
The cloudless skies, call not amiss,
For ev'ry nobler thought that stirs
The heart of each true Son of hers.
Mine be the envied lot to sing
Of ev'ry fair and beauteous thing,
Not to be found in foreign strand,
But here within my native land.
I will not speak of Washington,
Since blame or praise there can be none,
Nor Henry, whose impetuous soul
Within him burn'd as living coal,
Whose tongue made colder natures feel
The warmth of his impassioned zeal,
Whose flaming words could burn their way

Thro' opposition, and convey
The warmth of that electric flame
Which thrill'd the source from whence it came.
These and a thousand yet beside
Might fully claim a poet's pride
To sing them all, but time demands
A later hero at my hands.

The blue Potomac rolls its way
Near where this hero saw the day,
Ancestral trees and oaks surround
This more to us than classic ground,
Where oft, no doubt, beneath their shade,
In youth, our coming hero played.
What Art and Nature could bestow
To make him great, she gave we know,
As fine a frame as well could grace
A mortal, and a noble face
Were his, and empire even now
Sat calmly on his regal brow,
No need of adventicus airs
To supplement what Nature spares.
A power we cannot define
Belongs to some by right divine;
For titles are but idle things
To fill the empty heads of Kings;
'Tis mind, superior to all,
Before which mortals freely fall.
Mind is indeed a spark of God
That permeates the senseless clod,
The more of it in man we see,
We feel the more like God is he,
Yet moral adjuncts must combine
Before the structure seems divine,
For intellect and mind alone
Are cold and cruel, save its own
It seeks no other good but fierce
W

It leads all weaker minds perverse,
Satan and all the hosts of Hell
Still kept their wisdom when they fell,
The fiend of darkness still portrays
His Maker's likeness in the blaze
Of wisdom almost infinite
Which in him shines in all its might.

Few are the names not born to die,
For Nature can but few supply.
How many brilliant wits have sped
To graves among the nameless dead,
That in their little day have shone
In spheres peculiarly their own ;
Like tiny meteors at night
That burst and dissipate, a light
That glows and in a moment dies,
Their duty fill'd—'twas but surprise ;
But comets in their course appear
But once in many a rolling year,
So is it in the world of mind
With those whose brilliance makes us blind
A moment, like the lightning's light
It leaves us in a deeper night ;
But stars there were whose light shall shine
While empires sicken and decline.
Such was the man whose fame must live
Beyond all titles man may give ;
Born as it were an age too late
To rightly serve his own, but fate,
Which is another name for him
Who made the glowing seraphim,
Knew best its mighty, vast design
In making him whose light shall shine
With lustre, brightening from the age
When first he came upon the stage.

Scarce had he won on foreign shore
The laurels he so proudly bore
As tokens of his valor given,
Ere clouds had darken'd all the heaven.
The die was cast; no halting now.
Could treason sit on such a brow?
Ah no, and mortal never drew
With more regret a sword so true.
Beneath his country's flag he won
His early honors. How could one
So true as he had been before
Become a traitor; he forebore,
Gave pause, until he looked within
A heart whose purpose must have been
Serene and high. Let deeds attest
No malice rankled in his breast:
The line was drawn; could he consent.
To shed his Mother's blood intent
Alone with mercenary aim?
Sought he new fields to win his fame?
Ah no, the darkest of his life
Was just before the fearful strife;
But, once deciding, was to do,
So for his own his sword he drew.
'Tis past! and we will not recount
The heights which he essay'd to mount,
How, 'mid all changes, he preserved
A purpose which he never swerved,
Without one thought of turning back
He held amain on Duty's track.
He died as only heroes die,
Of honors full, his deeds supply
An ample legacy to all;
A model for the great and small.
He liv'd for all; no factions claim
The prestige of his mighty name;

That name no heir-loom of a clan,
But common property of man.
Beneath the soil that gave him birth
He sleeps, and never Mother Earth
Receiv'd to her a nobler son
Than he, an almost peerless one.
So bright in war, in peace so fair,
E'en envy had no shafts to spare
To launch at him, but far above,
In peace and plenitude of love,
His name shall run the course of time,
In distance more and more sublime,
His spotless fame become more bright
As rolling years shall mark their flight.

LINES TO OUR POET, WALT.

Walt, tho' we feel it decidedly wrong
  For poets and painters to abuse one another,
More so in the sacred pavillions of song
  To lightly speak ill of a friend or a brother;

But Walter you know you lay all the claim
  To honors poetic this side of the water,
Longfellow is viewing his laurels with shame,
  While Bryant and others you slaughter.

A modern Columbus and a new world of song
  Are titles pretentious to which you lay claim,
And one would believe, as you saunter along,
  You not only discover'd, but inhabit the same.

Now, while we allow some choice expressions
    Are found in your books, yet these are all marred
By so much that is trashy (these are honest confessions)
    'Tis queer how they ever fille l the mind of a bard.

Nastiness never can furnish the Muses
    With nectar, that dainty from above must be given ;
An animal is known by the food that he uses,
    And the bread may be spoil'd by profusion of leaven.

We have look'd at your features in hopes to discern
    Some twinklings of genius in your lustreless eyes,
Some poetical Etna, whose fires must burn
    And flash thro' the craters which nature supplies.

But tho' your physique doth set at defiance
    All claims to a genius, perhaps you are sent
To teach us poor mortals there can be no reliance
    On any hypothesis that man may invent.

Herculean in body, Miltonic in mind,
    A mountain in one, in the other a peak,
How can we poor devils, so puny and blind,
    E'er rightly conjecture such a wonderful freak ?

Disappointed in this, we have turn'd to your book,
    To your volume entitled the " Leaves of the Grass,"
But could not divine with the plummet we took
    To rate you a genius, or pronounce you an ass.

That you have a kind heart no one will deny,
    Your kindness will ever be a proof as to this,
But the eagle alone is permitted to fly
    And gaze on the sun, poets frequently miss.

In order therefore as a means of success,
  Do'nt speak so disdainfully, your wings may be leather,
And you may desire some day in distress
  To find in a chimney a home from the weather.

So the world is divided in opinion you see,
  Some call you a genius, others rate you an ass;
My private opinion, you surely must be
  A mixture of both, (vide your fondness for " Grass.")

And Walter, besides, you've set up to shoot at
  Yourself as a mark, and a sensible Owl
Who wishes to hoot suffers others to hoot at,
  Or else we would call him a very queer fowl.

But not one tittle would we ever detract
  From that lofty opinion you may entertain Walt
Of yourself, tho' we are aware of the fact
  That mutton and beef both spoil without salt.

SUCCESS.

SUGGESTED BY THE ISSUE OF THE WAR.

What is success?   Does it alone consist
  In ends accomplish'd, tho' black as night they be?
The World says so; and he who aim'd but missed
  A noble object cannot deserve to be
Call'd a successful man, at least by those
Who cannot tell a toad-stool from a rose.

He who hath labor'd, tho' it be in vain,
　(In vain alone to those who cannot see
The beauty of truth) is destin'd yet to gain
　The riches true that take no wings and flee,
Co-workers with God in his stupendous plan
To raise and dignify his fellow-creature, Man.

Is there nothing real?　Are there not any
　· Who may be honest, upright and pure, ·
A noble few among the vulgar many
　Whose skirts are clear and have not gloated o'er,
A brother's blood, nor thrust, a lying tongue
Into his name, or done him fouler wrong?

Ah yes, there are indeed a noble few
　Exceptions! call them from the motley throng,
Who either know not what they say and do,
　Or knowing, meaner still, delight in wrong.
Success with them doth equal meaning claim,
Tho' it end in crime or, result in shame.

How oft we hear that word miscall'd, success,
　Ill-gotten gains by villainy and fraud
Are winning cards, a genius to possess
　No matter how, a blessing from the Lord,
Intellect, genius, the riches of the mind,
Are prized by few, these few seldom we find.

Vain hypocrites, who would that we believe
　The lie that damns yourselves, believe not we
Can e'er for truth your knavish tricks receive,
　Say we were wrong, and bend a pliant knee.
Let those eat dirt whose very natures crave
No higher boon than what befits a slave.

How more than true seems ev'ry word that came
From Roland's lips as she to death was lead:
"Oh, Liberty, what crimes are foster'd in thy name!"
Thy robes are steep'd in blood, the countless dead,
Who in thy cause their noble lives have given,
Would form a holocaust as high as Heaven!

TO A NOTED PHILANTHROPIST.

Tho' I have never pressed thy hand,
  Have never heard thy friendly voice,
Yet millions in this goodly land
  Will e'en at thy name rejoice.

No parasites thy spirit needs,
  'Tis joy itself and needs no aid,
Its joy to heal the wound that bleeds,
  Its triumph when the wound is staid.

What if titles, flattery, fame,
  Are born to some, 'twas thine to know
A higher source than pride of name,
  The power to sweeten cups of woe.

I know not that thine eyes shall trace
  These feeble lines, which come so free
From out my heart, yet Heaven's grace
  Preserve Thee long, (My prayer for Thee.)

REMORSE.

It ne'er was intended the body should control
  And rivet in chains the free-born spirit.
Conquest, save thro' love, was ne'er for the soul:
  Matter alone that meanness should inherit.
'Tis baser, more than perfidy to yield
The mind to matter on an equal field.

'Tis sad to retrospect a human life,
  Misspent it may be thro' one mistake
Made ere we knew the future could be rife,
  And that results unending their currents take
Toward Destiny itself; one little lapse
Creates a world, miscalled in phrase, " perhaps."

Who at his age would even dare to turn
  His eye to Heaven nor feel a sense of shame,
Who has a heart that does not throb and burn
  With its own repining, nor his lips proclaim
Oh, God! without the mercy of thy Son,
My soul, my soul, were utterly undone.

INHERITED SIN.

As I lay on my pillow reviewing,
  The deeds of my wicked young life,
A thought that is e'er pursuing
  Saddened me with horror so rife.

The sins of the Father must fall
  On the head of his innocent child ;

If the Father, were vicious then all,
   On his soul, like a mountain, is piled.

No power in Heaven will save
   The soul that inherits the sin
Of a parent perhaps in his grave
   Beyond all atonement therein.

The evils that claim him their own
   Seeming grinning with ghastly delight
At a captive whose bitt'erest groan
   No mercy can claim. Is it right?

But God is all love I believe,
   Tho' I die by the sins of another,
And its import wait to receive,
   But not in this world, but the other.

SELF-CONSCIOUSNESS.

It hath been said that ev'ry heart
   Hath its own sorrow; this is true,
Man hath a good and better part—
   A Devil and an Angel too.

Imagination bodies forth
   Some beams from man's celestial sky,
Yet even there the soul is loth
   To part with, or to let them fly.

What, then, are all the arts of style
   But trappings wherewith truth to hide?
Man in his heart is far too vile,
   Fools only throw the veil aside.

GOOD-BYE.

———

Here ends the book. Indulgent reader spare
Its many faults alike of style and measure.
As to the critics, you know what critics are,
For without faults what were the critic's pleasure ?

If in its pages thy kindly eye hath found
One solitary thought which made thee pause,
To mark its beauty, my object has been crowned
With something dearer than undeserved applause.

Good-bye! Committed to thy mind I leave
My own best thoughts; deal with them as you may,
And whether I a world's applause receive
Or not, the book is written, and begins its day.